THE SPIDER:
THE CITY THAT PAID TO DIE

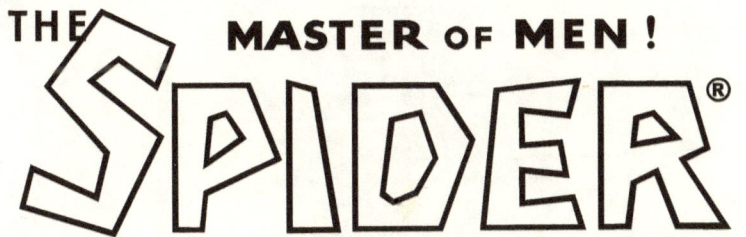

MASTER OF MEN!

THE CITY
THAT PAID TO DIE

By Grant Stockbridge

POPULAR PUBLICATIONS • 2022

CHAPTER 1
MASSACRE!

RICHARD WENTWORTH slapped the police commissioner's desk with an emphatic palm. He did not mince words. "Don't be so confoundedly blind, Kirk!" he said vehemently.

Commissioner Stanley Kirkpatrick knuckled his waxed mustache, masking a smile. "This is really quite a compliment, Dick," he said dryly. "You don't usually appeal to the police for help in criminal matters."

A sharp impatience goaded Wentworth, but he held himself rigidly in check. The charges he had come to make were not susceptible of proof. Good God, how could a man prove that a state and city government were in the hands of criminals! But the indications were there, plain at least to Wentworth's keen mind.

He said quietly, "Have your fun while you can, Kirk. You're accusing me again of being the Spider. While you delay, more infamies are being planned."

Kirkpatrick's smile persisted. He had long been convinced that Wentworth was the lone wolf of justice who called himself the Spider, who fought criminals with a ruthless hand, finding his own verdicts, administering his own executions inexorably—a master of men at once feared and respected. But proof had never fallen into his hands, and Wentworth and Kirkpatrick

were warm friends. Not that this fact would swerve Kirkpatrick from the path of duty by a hair's breadth if ever he found evidence....

Wentworth's own lips twisted into a smile that was cold, almost hostile. "I'll tell you this," he said slowly. "If the Spider shared my knowledge of the things that have been done by the police in the last thirty days, and if he knew your true nature less

2

This truck was only the first in the procession
which filed through the streets.

thoroughly, there could be only one ending for Police Commissioner Stanley Kirkpatrick!"

Kirkpatrick's smile vanished, "What the hell are you talking about?"

"A little red seal," Wentworth said softly. "A small red seal shaped like a spider which sometimes is found on the foreheads of the criminals the Spider brings to justice. I say, if the Spider knew what I do, *that seal would be found on your forehead*—and you would be dead!"

Kirkpatrick snapped to his feet and blood stained his saturnine cheeks darkly. "Wentworth!" he cried. "Are you accusing me of treachery? Why, damn you…."

"That's better," Wentworth nodded, his chiseled lips moving in a faint smile. "Now you can hear what I say. You weren't really listening before. What I said was this: The police department is being used to protect and foster crime. This so-called Party of Justice, which swept the city and the state last election, is governed by criminals and used by them for personal profit. And the police… Almost anyone else, Kirk, would blame you to the extent of believing you crooked. As it is, I say you're confoundedly blind!"

THE TWO men confronted each other angrily, both strong, arrogant, dominant. Kirkpatrick was a little older, as the silvering of his temples attested; his face more square cut and stern. Wentworth's lips were shaped for laughter, and there was always mockery in the quirk of his smooth black brows—a face of quick intelligence, of keen determination. Both men were idealists; both leaders. Natural friends… or enemies.

The effort Kirkpatrick made at self-control was plain in the

4

white lines that cut about his mouth. He turned abruptly away to the window. Wentworth strode after him, clasped a hand on his shoulder.

"I apologize for goading you, Kirk," he said, his voice deepening, "but, believe me, I do not exaggerate. The morals of the force is broken. Your men are slipping up, deliberately, in their duty. Criminals get away with things they would not have dared attempt before."

Kirkpatrick's intonation was still stiff. "You must have reason for what you say, Wentworth. This Party of Justice—?"

"Have you been reappointed commissioner yet, Kirk?" Wentworth interrupted.

Kirkpatrick shook his long head slowly. "I have seen Mayor Culkin twice. He is… delaying."

"Delaying, yes. You won't be reappointed, Kirk. Four successive administrations have reappointed you, but not Mayor Culkin. Kirk, you remember how much money was lavished on that campaign? You know the trend of state and city government since then."

Kirkpatrick faced about slowly. "It seems sound enough. Business, industry, and capital has been relieved of many of the taxes. Labor has fallen into line. We're headed for a prosperous era, without a doubt. This talk of criminals…."

"Criminals have been used—" Wentworth pounded home his point—"to work the will of the men behind the Party of Justice. They were protected. Now they are getting out of hand. When they are strong enough, they will… eliminate the men behind the Party of Justice and take it over for themselves!"

He demanded, "God, Kirk, can't you see the danger? The public officials were put in office as puppets—to take orders. They can be handled and controlled just as readily by criminals as by the financiers who back the Party of Justice. How long do you think it will take criminals to realize that?"

Kirkpatrick's frown made a worried crease between his brows. "You keep referring to the men behind the party. Are there any such men? Do you know?"

"I'll tell you three of them," Wentworth said shortly. "Legislation has been aimed at the relief of the utilities controlled by Angus Whitfield; of the factories of Malcolm Nicol; the holding companies of Martin Ducamps!"

Kirkpatrick moved a hand impatiently, "That's guess-work," he said shortly. "You have no proof—"

The shrilling of the telephone upon his desk cut short his words, and he reached the instrument in a stride, snapped it to his ear.

"Kirkpatrick speaking," he said, then his eyes whipped to those of Wentworth. "Martin Ducamps is calling!" he repeated blankly.

In a stride, Wentworth had caught up an extension phone in the desk customarily used by Kirkpatrick's secretary. He heard the rasping, dictatorial tones of the financier.

"… protection at once," he was saying. "We are at conference at my office. Ducamps Building. We have been threatened. I'll give you the details now, in case… This fool uses a trick mirror. He appears as a—" Ducamps' voice paused for a moment, went on in a lower tone, almost a whisper—"a white face in the mirror, and in that way he conceals—"

Ducamps' voice broke off in a hoarse scream of mortal agony, and over the wire there came the heavy, stuttering thunder of a machine gun. There were other screams, a louder crash and the phone went dead! In a long leap, Wentworth reached Kirkpatrick's desk, slapped open a cam on the annunciator.

"Radio operator!" he said sharply. "Emergency wagon and all near-by patrol cars to Ducamps Building. Ducamps' offices. A wholesale murder. And fast, man, fast! Order the building closed up completely. No one goes in or out. Send reserves from the nearest stationhouse. That is all."

He straightened. "Forgive me, Kirk," he said, "for usurping authority. It saved a few seconds."

Kirkpatrick was on his feet. He whipped a long-barreled .38 revolver from his drawer, thrust it into his belt. "Right," he said curtly. "Order my car—to the front door. Headquarters homicide detail to follow. Every man they've got."

IT WAS while Kirkpatrick and Wentworth strode through the halls, side by side, that the commissioner spoke, almost angrily. "You're right again, Dick," he said sharply, "and I'm wrong. God grant that we're in time at least."

Wentworth's lips were grimly set but he had no such hope. The murderers must have known that Ducamps was talking to police headquarters, that the alarm would be instantaneous. They would lose no time in escaping from the building. But Wentworth's voice was calm as Kirkpatrick's personal car sirened its way southward through traffic.

"I had time to give you only part of my reasons for suspecting those three men, Ducamps, Nicol and Whitfield. Not that I think they are the only ones. The tax bill that is up at Albany today is an incredible measure. It puts ninety percent of the burden on the lower and middle brackets of income—leaves the big-money men almost tax-free. I have Jackson up there, and he reports that the law carries a rider which would empower tax collectors to seize property of any kind, without waiting for delinquency—unless the tax is paid on demand."

Kirkpatrick said, "My God, Dick. Nothing like that has been printed in the newspapers!"

Wentworth shook his head with a thin smile on his lips. "I think we should add another name to our list, the man who secretly controls most of the newspapers in the state—Howard Soldan. We don't know how many men were in this conference of Ducamps', but God help the people of this state if criminals have seized control from the crooked officials who have been using them for their own purposes."

Kirkpatrick said thickly, "God help them, yes, if He can. Dick, I have been blind... *blind*, I tell you!"

There were a dozen blue-coated police about the Ducamps Building when Kirkpatrick's limousine slid to a halt there. A sergeant saluted.

"Twenty-first floor, Commissioner," he reported. "There's seven men dead up there."

Kirkpatrick nodded curtly. He did not speak, but the thinning of his lips told the shock of those words. Wentworth's swift eyes canvassed the crowd jammed in the lobby of the building by the police. A raft of office workers, clerks and stenographers. Nor was there any reason for suspecting one more than another.

"Upstairs first," Kirkpatrick said.

The directors' room of Ducamps' offices was a shambles. Ducamps' seat had been at the head of the table, and bullets had clawed through the back of the chair, drilled his body in a dozen places. A phone was shattered under his hand. It was plain that the other men had attempted to escape in vain. Wentworth's face went grim at the sight. He was no stranger to death, yet violence could stir him. The very fact of the attack upon these men was proof enough of the things that Wentworth had deduced and reported to Kirkpatrick.

The bullets had come from behind Ducamps... Wentworth swore softly under his breath, as his eyes centered on a curious mirror that hung on the wall. From that, his gaze swept over the room, gauging the paths of bullets.

"Kirk," he said softly, "the bullets came from that mirror."

Kirkpatrick's head jerked toward him. "From that mirror?" he said blankly. "How could they?"

Wentworth shook his head, crossed until he could peer into the mirror itself. He could discern no break in its concave surface, but he was sure. It had to be that.

"What was it Ducamps said?" Wentworth asked quietly, and his voice dropped in imitation of the man speaking over the phone. *"White face in the mirror...."*

There was a faint clicking sound. Before Wentworth's narrowed, watching eyes, a narrow port irised open in the middle of that concave glass.

"To the floor!" Wentworth shouted. "Flat on the floor, every man!"

He hurled himself in a long, headlong dive at Kirkpatrick's legs and, in the same instant, the furious, deadly stammer of a machine gun thundered into the room!

CHAPTER 2
MIRROR OF DEATH

ONCE MORE, as over the telephone, men's dying screams rang terribly through the long, lavish room. Some of the investigators in the room had heeded Wentworth's shouted hoarse command, but others had waited to look about, to find the reason for that call. They never did. The sweeping stream of bullets hosed from that swiveling machine gun scythed them down.

Wentworth's dive drove his shoulder against Kirkpatrick's thighs, hammered him back against the wall and to the floor. Instantly, Wentworth released his hold and, flat on his back, he drew his automatic with the swift, deadly precision for which he was known and dreaded. It blasted in his hand, jerking with the recoil, dropping back into line with the mechanical perfection of a machine, but fast... fast. Starred holes were sewn across the mirror, three above, three below that deadly port. The first shot had smashed squarely upon the muzzle. Behind the mirror, there was another muffled blast, and after that the gun fell silent.

In the instant it ceased, Wentworth was on his feet, charging. Behind him screams still shrilled. There were the hoarse

angry shouts of frightened men. A second, loaded automatic was in Wentworth's left hand now. It was with the empty in his right that he struck the mirror. It splintered, tinkled in musical shards to the floor, and Wentworth swore harshly, monotonously under his breath. He had uncovered a recess in the wall, a machine gun clamped into a device that still was swinging the shattered muzzle easily from side to side—a murder-trap deadly in its simple efficiency. Quite obviously, it had been started electrically through a sonic device actuated by the words he had uttered in echo of Ducamps' own mortal phrase, *"White face in the mirror."*

Kirkpatrick, shaken and drawn of face, came swiftly to his side. Through a long moment, he stared into the recess, then he strode to the door. "Doctor Elliott!" he called to the medical examiner. "Come quickly. There may be some..." He turned back toward the room. The screams had ceased. Among the three policemen who had fallen, there was no sign of life at all.

Wentworth said fiercely, "I'm a blundering fool! I should have guessed...."

Kirkpatrick said, heavily. "No blame attaches to you, Dick. You couldn't possibly know. And you saved five lives, not counting my own. Those people on the first floor—"

"It will do no good to question them," Wentworth said shortly. "This trap could have been set a week ago. That's a hundred-shot drum. It was rigged to fire half of those when first those key words were uttered. That would be easy. A magnet to pull back the trigger and hold it there for a stipulated time. It's possible some of the employees here will know who had access to this room. Because of the mirror, I imagine entrance was restricted."

Their questioning revealed that Ducamps allowed no one save himself in the conference chamber, except on days when a conference was held. Once, a week before, Governor Whiting and he had been closeted in there for an hour. Afterward, the governor had worked there alone....

Kirkpatrick and Wentworth stared at each other incredulously. Governor Whiting!

"It's impossible," Kirkpatrick said shortly.

"I agree," Wentworth said softly. "Whiting is only a puppet. Nevertheless, the answer to this puzzle lies in Albany right now. Whoever is behind this massacre will lose no time in asserting his authority over Governor Whiting and the legislature. Kirk… could you pretend to play along with Mayor Culkin and the others?"

Kirkpatrick's drawn face was very pale. He dragged a palm down heavily over his eyes. "Pretend? I don't know, Dick. I can try, perhaps. Why?"

Wentworth explained rapidly. There was no doubt that Kirkpatrick was slated for dismissal. Once he was removed, the police would be completely in the hands of the criminals behind Culkin and Governor Whiting—and it would be damnably difficult for Kirkpatrick to regain his position.

"If you could stay in power," Wentworth said swiftly, "and

stall for time until we can locate the criminals behind this atrocity, you would be in a position to strike when the moment came. Out of office…."

"Out of office," Kirkpatrick said slowly, "I am only another and less efficient Wentworth. And the Spider needs no allies."

Wentworth smiled, thin-lipped. God knew the Spider would need all his strength and more to combat an organization as well entrenched as the criminal who, this moment, was seizing control of the state!

"I'll do the best I can, Dick," Kirkpatrick said grimly, "but I'll consent to no criminality!"

Wentworth's hand closed on Kirkpatrick's shoulder. "Good," he said heartily. "If I learn anything, I'll communicate, but not by phone. I'm sure you're watched all the time. Now, if you'll authorize me to go out through your cordon downstairs…."

Kirkpatrick strode beside him. "Do you have any plans, Dick? By God, I'd like to go with you! Anything to strike a blow at these damned murderers!"

"Your job is here," Wentworth said slowly, and regretfully. It would be good to have such an ally as Kirkpatrick beside him, for no one realized better than he the incredible proportions of the task ahead. "I'm going to Albany and register a protest again the tax—personally, with Governor Whiting!"

Kirkpatrick held out his hand. "Good luck," he said and his voice was harsh. "God knows, you'll need it!"

WENTWORTH CAUGHT a taxi back to his home behind Sutton Place, the walled fortress of a mansion which he had built partly on filled land between two East River piers. His

RICHARD
WENTWORTH

eyes were gloomy with foreboding; and the sunshine that occasionally struck down through the glass roof of the cab, seemed an incongruous thing. The proud skyscrapers, were strangely serene against the blue of the sky, the hustling crowds on the street totally unaware of the peril that hung over them. Every man and woman of the multitude would soon feel the weight of criminal depredations unless... God in Heaven, what could one man accomplish, even though that man was the Spider?

His arms pressed against the accustomed bulge of the automatics beneath his arm. He could kill. His lips twisted ironically. It was his destiny that he who loved humanity so must prove his love by... murder. But he had never killed an innocent man. Before those guns could blast, he would find the keystone of the arch of criminal power which imprisoned the state. He must find the guilty men, without fail. That was the real purpose of his trip to Albany. He would protest against the tax, yes, but in a special and dangerous way. As so often before, he would offer his person as a sacrifice, a murder bait for the criminals....

The taxi swerved to the curb on Sutton Place, and Wentworth

strode into one of the houses that abutted the street on the East. He walked swiftly through a first-floor apartment, entered a clothes closet and manipulated certain hooks. The floor moved gently downward—a platform elevator—and he was in a narrow concrete corridor. At its far end, he entered another elevator and was whisked up to the third floor of his fortress mansion. He stepped out into a hallway whose marble walls masked armor plate. He had been under periscope observation since he had entered that other apartment. Now, a bronze-covered door flung wide and a turbaned, bearded Sikh greeted him with a low salaam.

"Any further reports from Jackson?" Wentworth asked curtly.

The dark-faced Sikh's voice came out with a strong nasal accent. *"Han, sahib!* It is recorded."

Wentworth strode directly to the recording device and listened to the playback of the telephone report. The voice of his man, Jackson, stationed in Albany since Wentworth's suspicions had centered on Governor Whiting, came to him crisply, but with curt overtones of worry.

"On receipt of news from New York of the deaths of seven wealthy men and three police," Jackson reported. "Governor Whiting took a personal message to the legislature. He proposed to establish a New York Bureau of Investigation to parallel the federal G-men. They would be uniformed and have powers transcending those of local or state police. The bill was passed by both houses as an emergency measure with an appropriation of a million dollars, and Governor Whiting, within thirty minutes, swore in Jervis Strong as commandant of the NYBI.

Tax measure passed as reported. Collections already begun. Owners of two stores were flogged into producing money and their stores emptied of all valuable goods. This will not appear in the newspapers."

With a tautening of his entire body, Wentworth heard that succinct and barren report. The anger that he had held in check now swelled through him hotly. He would be too late to protest the tax, and this police law was damnable. Like the other measures, it was excellent on the face of it. But "transcendent powers," greater than those of the local police, had been granted, and in criminal hands, that was a fearful weapon. The dishonesty behind the measure was plainly evident, too, in Governor Whiting's appointment of the commandant Jervis Strong!

Damn it, Jervis Strong was a criminal for all that he had no police record. He had been too clever for that, but Wentworth had personal knowledge that the man had been tied in with big-time racketeers during and after prohibition. And now he was to head a powerful police force for a criminal-ruled governor! For one fierce moment, Wentworth considered the expedience of removing these crooked officials—by death!

BUT THE Spider was no callous executioner. Whiting might be no more than weak and misled, the tool of some more powerful man. He was dangerous, but against such as those the Spider's guns were holster-bound. The governor might even be innocent of criminal intent, ill-advised. But Jervis Strong!... The thought flashed through Wentworth's keen mind that Strong might possibly be the power behind the throne, the man who had plotted this swift subjugation of the state. It was a thing he would investigate. He whipped toward his Sikh servitor.

"Have the radio truck I prepared ready in fifteen minutes," he ordered curtly. "See that the button-hole microphone and other equipment I'll need to broadcast to the truck is in it."

"Han, sahib!" The Sikh's dark eyes glowed with eagerness. "Thy servant goes with his master into battle?"

Wentworth smiled faintly. He might flinch from the lives he was forced to extinguish to protect the people, but for Ram Singh all battle was pure pleasure.

"The *missie sahib* must be guarded, my warrior," he said softly. "Here is where the greatest danger lies. Where I go, there will be only words, words."

Ram Singh acknowledged his orders with a low salaam, but there was disappointment in his eyes. Wentworth strode to a phone and put through a call to the apartment of the one woman in the world who shared his dangers and his secrets—even the dread secret that could destroy him, his work as the Spider. In a space of moments, her warm voice was in his ear.

"Nita, dear," he said, "I would be most happy if you could run over for a few minutes—at once." His language was curiously formal, and it had its special code significance for them both.

It meant that danger overhung them; that Wentworth was going into battle and Nita van Sloan would be in peril, too! Many times, his enemies had struck at him through his love. It was always his precaution that she should be domiciled in his fortress while he fought.

Nita's tones changed, but she said nothing to indicate the

danger of which she was instantly aware. Wentworth's phone and her own had been tapped before this.

"You are a most demanding fiancé," she said lightly. "I must drop everything at your lightest command! This one time, I'll humor you!"

Wentworth laughed. "You are too good to me, dear," he said.

That was all, but Wentworth hummed lightly beneath his breath as he went about the swift preparations for his departure. He waited only to tell Nita van Sloan swiftly of the things he feared and suspected, then he entered the truck Ram Singh had prepared for him and sped swiftly away through the city. In an hour, it would be dark. He would lose valuable time driving, instead of flying to Albany, but the radio equipment was essential to his plans. He wore a visored cap, a whipcord uniform, and on the side of the truck was painted the legend—*Amalgamated Parcel Delivery.*

It was a thin disguise, but, with the guns that nestled beneath his arms, Wentworth reinforced it against the criminals. If they should guess his identity and attack… Wentworth's lips grew thin with angry determination. God help those who stood in his way, for tonight the Spider struck his first blow against the criminal overlords of the state! This damnable forced immediate collection of taxes was a return to medieval ages….

THE STATE had lost no time in setting tax collectors to work under the new law. There was no time to put an experienced body of workers in the field, but there were more than a score of trained executives on hand, waiting for the law to be passed. Max Boyar went to Poughkeepsie, routed out the local officials and showed his credentials.

"This burg's quota under the new tax is a half million," he told the three men under him, briskly. "We'll pick up a truck and start the rounds tonight. They's shops open all over town. And listen to me, punks. When I give orders, you hop, see? I'm not giving them twice!"

Jack Wilson was new to his job in the tax office. He'd been there a month, to be precise, and he needed the work and the salary. He nodded slowly, unwillingly, to those strange orders. There couldn't be any doubt about the man's official credentials.

"Why do we need the truck?" he asked.

Max Boyar took a quick stride forward and his right hand slid under his coat lapel. "Getting balky already?" he asked softly.

Jack Wilson's head came up and blood stained his cheeks, angry blood. But he needed the job. "No, sir," he said quietly. "Shall I hire the truck?"

"Hire nothing!" Boyar snarled. "Tell 'em it's for the state tax department. Here's a badge." He tossed a glittering nickel shield on the desk. "Hop to it."

Jack Wilson's head came up and blood went out stiffly, without speaking again. There was a vertical frown between his brows. This Boyar was a funny sort of man to be appointed tax collector, he thought. He didn't know Max Boyar was a highly trained expert. Strong-arm men in the rackets have to know how to squeeze money out of reluctant people....

Tony Manteo's grocery was his home, too. There was a curtained door at the rear and, just beyond that, was the living-room. The radio was playing softly. Tony was happy. Tonight, he was honored by a visit from Father Fiorentia—Father Flower. Angela, his motherless daughter, was pouring the red wine for them.

"Angela, she is *bella*, beautiful, no?" Tony laughed. "She will make some man a fine wife, no? Another glass of wine for the good father, Angela *mia.*"

Father Flower smiled, and Angela laughed, too. Her dark hair was lustrous and color was dusky in her cheeks. She poured the glass of wine and, in the grocery, a little bell set on a spring above the door made a tinkling note. She pushed through the curtains to attend to the customer.

In the middle of the store, Max Boyar turned slowly on his heel, scanning the shelves, the dangling cheeses and stockfish. At his side, Jack Wilson still frowned. The others were out in the truck, waiting.

"You want something?" Angela asked.

Jack Wilson said, uncomfortably, "We're tax collectors. This is Mr. Boyar."

Boyar grunted, "How're ya, babe? You run this dump?"

The girl's dark eyes widened a little. "You will want my father," she said. "Excuse me, I...."

"Stick around, babe," Boyar said expansively. "Hey, Tony! Come out here and be damned quick about it."

Angela looked from Boyar's squat, powerful stance to Jack Wilson. Beyond the curtains, Tony's feet made quick, excited

21

sounds on the floor. He batted aside the curtains, then stopped. His eyes, too, swept past Boyar to Jack Wilson. Jack shifted uncomfortably. He explained again, mentioned Boyar's name.

Boyar fixed his small hard eyes on Tony Manteo. "There's a new tax been passed up at Albany," he said. "Your bill is two hundred dollars." He whipped a pad of forms out of his pocket, scribbled on it and shoved it at Tony. "I'll take your check."

Tony Manteo's face was blank with surprise. "Two hundred dollar," he said woodenly. He took the slip of paper. "Santa Maria! For why, two hundred dollar? What is this tax? I do not understand."

Boyar said softly, "So you're going to pull that stall, are you?"

Wilson took a quick step forward. "Please, Mr. Boyar," he said anxiously. "Let me explain to them. Mr. Manteo, an emergency law was passed up in Albany today. A special tax for relief. Mr. Boyar has been sent down to take charge of collection and he— he has assessed you for two hundred dollars."

Tony Manteo shook his head. "For why, two hundred dollars?" he cried. Angela moved to his side and held his arm.

In the curtained doorway, Father Flower's black robe showed. He stepped into the room quietly, his round ruddy face still gently smiling. His blue eyes were kindly, even when they rested on Boyar.

Boyar caught Wilson by the shoulder and yanked him back. "All right, Tony," he said shortly. "You've had your explanation. Now shell out!"

Tony's shoulders slumped a little. "If it is the law," he said humbly, "I must pay, yes. When must this tax be paid, please?"

"Right now, punk!"

"Now?" Tony cried. "Santa Maria, but I do not have it! What kind of tax is this that I must pay now?"

Angela said, "Surely, there is some mistake. I've never heard of a tax like that." Father Flower came wholly into the store, "There must be some mistake, surely," he said gently.

"Button your lip!" Boyar snapped at him. He took his hand out of his pocket, and a blackjack dangled from his wrist. "Do you pay, Tony, or do I clean out your store and smash your jaw in the bargain?"

The priest stepped in front of Tony Manteo and his daughter, the smile on his lips. "You are the most peculiar tax collector," he said quietly. "I think I'll have to see your credentials."

"You'll see nothing!" Violently, Boyar thrust the priest aside, slammed him up against the counter. A stack of canned foods tumbled and rolled on the floor.

Wilson's jaw set, "See here, Boyar!" he said sharply.

Boyar grabbed Manteo by the collar and jerked him forward. "Shell out!" he said grimly.

ANGELA DARTED past him with a movement as lithe as a cat's. She sprang for the door, but Boyar was too quick for her. The blackjack flicked out. It caught the girl just above the ear, and her dark hair swung wildly at the jar. She crumpled in a heap on the floor.

Manteo exploded. He swung awkward fists at Boyar, shouting in Italian. The blackjack came down twice, heavily, on Manteo's shoulders, and his arms went limp at his sides. Twice more the blackjack flicked home, across Manteo's face. Boyar prided

23

himself on being an artist with the blackjack. His blows did not put Manteo out. They only broke his nose and cut open his cheek.

Jack Wilson was stunned by the violence through those swift seconds, but now he sprang forward. His hand clamped on Boyar's shoulder and he swung him about into a chopping right jab that carried all Wilson's weight behind it Boyar's head snapped up and he pitched to the floor.

Jack took Tony Manteo gently by the arm and led him toward the door. "You go get a policeman right away," he said. "There's something fishy about this whole business. The state couldn't have sent a man like Boyar to collect taxes. It just isn't possible. Hurry! I'll look after Angela."

He swung back into the store. The priest was adjusting his habit. His lips were moving silently. On the floor, Boyar was sitting up slowly. His eyes focused on Jack, and red rage flared in them. With a movement, swift as the strike of a snake, his hand darted beneath his coat lapel and whipped out a revolver.

"Hit me, will you?" he demanded hoarsely. He got slowly to his feet "Hit me, will you?"

Jack, gazing into the man's twisted, fierce face, knew with sudden certainty that Boyar was going to shoot! He was dazed. Incredulous. He saw the gun fall into line on his body and his lips flew open in a gasp of protest, but all his body seemed paralyzed.

"Take it, then, you dumb cluck!" Boyar said venomously. His knuckles whitened from pressure. The hammer of the revolver was rearing back… Out of his eye corners, Jack saw the priest's arm move like a black flail. Boyar glimpsed it, too, spun and fired—but too late. One of the fallen cans of foodstuffs caught him in the side of the head and hammered him to the floor!

There was a gentle smile on Father Flower's lips. "The poor misguided man," he said softly. He got down on his knees beside Boyar and stroked the black sprawling hair back from his forehead. "I do think, though, that you'd better take his gun."

Out in the street, Tony Manteo's voice was lifted shrilly. Other voices sounded and the pounding feet of an assembling crowd. Angela was struggling to her feet, a palm pressed to her head. Jack Wilson helped her up.

"It's all right," he said hurriedly. "It's all right now." He put his arms around her and her uncertain head rested for a moment on her shoulder. "Your father's gone to get the police."

Father Flower's lips were moving again, but this time audibly. He was praying for forgiveness for his anger!

Wilson's thoughts were whirling. Boyar's credentials were entirely right, he told himself again, and he remembered that an emergency tax was pending. Damn it! What could such things mean! A state official behaving like a gangster....

"It's all right," he said woodenly again to the girl. "It has to be, or else...."

His voice broke off, and his head turned toward the door. The police would straighten things out... Jack Wilson's eyes widened. These were not Poughkeepsie police—these men in dapper black uniforms with heavy automatics on their hips. The man with sergeant's chevron's glittering in gold upon his arm, strode sharply forward into the store. There were three other men behind him and one of them had his fist twisted into Tony Manteo's collar!

"So you beat up a state official, did you?" said the sergeant. "This will get you about ten years. All right, boys, round up the lot and take them to jail. I'll look after Boyar."

Jack Wilson shook himself out of his befuddlement. "Look here, Sergeant," he said angrily, "they didn't resist Boyar. He took out his blackjack and started beating up Tony Manteo. He hit the priest, knocked the girl down."

The sergeant swung around toward Wilson. "Oh, a traitor, eh?" he sneered. "Lying on your own superior!" He jerked Angela out of Jack's arms and thrust her toward his men. Before Jack realized the sergeant's intention, his gun was out of its holster.

"Just hold that crowd back, boys," the sergeant said softly. "I think I'll have to teach this young punk a lesson before we take him in."

As he finished speaking, the gun whipped over and caught Jack on the temple. He reeled, fell to his knees, and the pistol lifted again like flail. When a gun crashed out, Jack Wilson thought, for a dazed moment, that he had been shot. The sergeant cursed and wrung his suddenly empty gun-hand. From the door a flat, mocking voice rang out.

"I don't think that's a good idea, Sergeant. I really don't!"

Jack saw the sergeant's eyes flare wide, saw his arms fly high as he backed away until his hips caught the counter. His mouth was working, but no words came out. Jack Wilson twisted his head about and saw the reason then.

One of the Black Police lay on the floor, unconscious. The

other two were crowded as close to the wall as they could get, hands high. And in the entrance-way crouched a figure shrouded in a long black cape; face taut and mocking under the broad brim of a black hat. In his fists were two heavy automatics. Their muzzles quested restlessly, covering the abject police.

The sergeant found his voice, in a whisper. "The Spider!" he gasped. "My God, the Spider!"

CHAPTER 3
CRIME'S LEGISLATURE

FURY ROWLED Wentworth as he confronted the Black Police in the tiny grocery. The gold NYBI badges on their chests were a mockery. These men enforce the law? They were strong-arm racketeers! They should be killed. Wentworth lifted his right gun. Never in his long career of fighting crime had the Spider turned his guns against the police, but these men....

Wentworth squeezed the trigger. His bullet raked across the sergeant's chest. The badge was ripped free, flew against the wall and fell, a battered, crumpled thing upon the floor. The sergeant's face was gray with terror, but his shaking hands remained high above his head.

"For God's sake, Spider!" he whimpered.

The Spider's left gun jerked twice and two more shields were bullet-torn from their wearer's chests. His voice came out, flat with menace.

"If I find anyone of you hiding again behind those shields," he said slowly, "I'll pin them to your hearts... with bullets! Understand? Now unbuckle your gun belts and get out of here. Fast!"

There was need enough for speed. The street was crowded with people. Wentworth was bitterly conscious of them behind his back. Probably they would be friendly, but among them, there might be one who wanted the glory of killing the Spider, even by means of a shot in the back. And other police might come....

"Hurry!" Wentworth snapped again. "And take your carrion with you!"

Actually, the Black Police needed no admonition to haste. Their hands trembled with eagerness to be gone. They caught up Boyar and their unconscious companion and staggered out of the door. Instantly, Wentworth sprang toward the others— toward Jack Wilson, Angela and the wounded grocer, the priest.

"Out the back way," he directed, in a whisper. "We must hurry!"

Each moment they delayed here, his personal peril, and theirs, increased. Wentworth had had no time for thorough disguise after the street crowd had indicated to him that already the myrmidons of the state's criminal rulers were at work here. His cape covered his chauffeur's uniform. The truck was parked on the back street. If they moved fast, they might make good their escape. How soon would the police spread their alarm....

Jack Wilson pushed himself up groggily from his knees. There was a smear of blood across his temple from the policeman's gun. Angela helped her father toward the curtained door of their living-room, but Father Flower regarded Wentworth with bright, interested eyes.

"I'm afraid, son," the priest said gently, "that you have made only additional trouble for yourself. Tony will be a marked man now."

"For me, it matters little enough, Father," Wentworth smiled as he moved toward the priest, "but we must get these others away. The police will return any moment now. You can no longer expect justice from the law. What would happen to you and these other three would... not be pretty. Lead the way, Father."

Father Flower bowed his head, and Wentworth herded them all through the little living-room, where the radio still played, toward the rear door. Jack Wilson hung back.

"I want to thank you, sir," he said. "I think that sergeant intended to kill me. I don't understand why. I don't understand any of this. I'm a tax collector here, deputy. But that man, Boyar, had orders from Albany. You said we could no longer expect justice from the law."

Jack Wilson had a hesitant smile that made his face curiously boyish. "I know, of course, that you're the Spider. I've... I've read about your wonderful work, and I never quite understood why the police hunted you."

"Later," Wentworth urged kindly. His hand closed on Jack Wilson's shoulder. "There is no time...."

Behind them, a man's voice sounded shrilly in the street. "Here come the cops! Beat it!"

"Hurry! There's a truck on the next street! Room for all of us!" Wentworth drove them before him at a shambling run, hurried them into the truck. Tony Manteo he stretched out full length in the aisle between the radio instruments that lined the walls of the back. Angela pillowed his head in her lap. Father Flower stepped back.

"God-speed," he said gravely.

Wentworth spun toward him. In spite of the man's mild exte-

The empty sedan charged half-way up steps of the Capitol!

rior, he recognized a steadfast purpose here. The priest knew his danger fully, but preferred to remain where duty dictated, though he must guess the brutality and injustice that threatened. Wentworth flung a glance toward the alleyway from which they had darted. No one there yet, but there were rough shouts in the distance.

"Tony needs you," Wentworth told the priest hurriedly. "I can't doctor him. No time. We don't dare stop for medical attention. His left collarbone is broken."

The priest's eyes were concerned. "You are providing me with an excuse to leave my plain duty," he said. "You are a curious man, Spider. I...."

The shouting was nearer. There was a shot, a woman's scream. "Hurry, Father!" Wentworth cried. "We won't leave without you." He drew his guns, checked them quietly. "If we remain, men will be killed. You can't sanction that, no matter what they are. And Tony needs you."

With a sigh and a shake of his head, Father Flower climbed into the truck beside Jack Wilson. "It is so difficult to be sure," he said, "and I have sinned already tonight in anger...."

The rest of his words were lost in the engine roar as the car leaped forward under the Spider's skillful hands. A shot rang out behind and a frosted star gleamed in the window glass beside him. The truck heeled far over as it screamed around a corner with mounting speed.

THE SPIDER'S false heavy brows were drawn together in a worried frown, and his gray-blue eyes kept vigilant watch on the road behind. So far no glare of pursuing headlights showed in his rear-vision mirror. Five times he doubled on his trail, heading ever southward. Now, he reversed his direction and sped northward through the outskirts of the city.

It was his hope that the police would think he was fleeing

toward New York City. He could not abandon the truck since it was tied in so closely with his plans in Albany. He glanced toward Jack Wilson, seated beside him while Father Flower and Angela worked over Tony. Wilson's young face was drawn into grim lines.

"You asked me about the police and the tax collector, Wilson," Wentworth said quietly. "They are authentic and fully empowered to do what they did. The truth is that criminals have control of the state government."

"Criminals!" Wilson's face sagged with amazement. "But that doesn't seem—"

"No," Wentworth agreed. "But it has happened—legally, so far as can be proved. The federal government has no more basis for intervention than it had when Huey Long controlled Louisiana. Some people said there was criminality there. I don't know. But those Black Police and the tax collector were acting within the limits of the new emergency laws passed at Albany. What I'm leading up to is this: Neither you, nor any of these others, will be safe in Poughkeepsie again. They will make an example of you to show others that they must bow down to the law."

Wilson shook his head. "Then Tony Manteo will lose his store. My job is gone too—"

"You escaped with your lives," Wentworth reminded him grimly. "There is a friend of mine in New York City—Richard Wentworth. I want you to buy a car with the money I'll give you presently. Take these others to Wentworth's home and stay there. There's a long fight ahead, unless… Well, you'll be safer there, and Wentworth will find work for you to do. Better to remain in hiding awhile."

Wilson said heavily, "I suppose there's nothing else to do."

Wentworth laughed sharply. "You're fortunate to

THEY DIDN'T PAY THE POOR TAX

have so safe a refuge. What you have seen tonight is only the beginning of the terror that will come!"

A half hour later, he saw Wilson and the others on their way, by a round-about route, toward New York City. Then he sped on, himself, toward Albany. It lacked an hour of midnight when he rolled across the bridge and pulled to a halt near a quick-lunch diner, in the river-side district of Albany. When he emerged five minutes later, a broad-shouldered man with a strangely military bearing followed him, and climbed into the seat beside him.

"I was beginning to worry, sir," he said quietly. "There's been no new development here except that they seem to have gangsters out to collect the taxes. Some of the things made my blood boil, sir, but your orders wouldn't allow me to interfere."

"You've done good work, Jackson," Wentworth said quietly. He was again in his chauffeur's uniform. "I was delayed in Poughkeepsie by some of that same… tax collecting. Where will I find the governor?"

"Sticking pretty close to the legislature, sir," Jackson said steadily. "He has set up an office in the building, and he's delivering a series of personal messages. He might be either place—in his office, or in the legislature."

"More deviltry!" Wentworth said sharply. "You'd think with those tax and police laws, they'd have enough for one day. Take the wheel, Jackson. Drive as near to the legislature as you think safe. I'm going to change my clothing in the back here. After I leave you, rig up this set for short-wave re-broadcast. Run up the telescopic antenna as high as possible and pick a place where you're not apt to get interference."

Jackson took the wheel of the truck. "You're going to use that portable broadcasting outfit, sir?"

Wentworth laughed harshly. "When I call on the governor," he said, "I'm going to be wired for sound. Every radio that's tuned to a short-wave station will bring in what he says and what I say! There's been too much secrecy. If the people know the truth, perhaps we can accomplish something toward smashing this damnable combine."

"It will be dangerous for you, sir."

Wentworth said, grimly. "It also will be dangerous for the governor—and anybody that gets in my way! Blanket as many wavebands as possible, Jackson. Full power!"

IT STILL lacked a half hour of midnight when Richard Wentworth, faultlessly tailored and carrying a large dispatch case, walked calmly up to the front steps of the Capitol. Lights blazed in the legislative chambers but, except for squads of Black Police, the corridors were deserted. Wentworth was acutely conscious of the guns beneath his arms, but his clothing had been carefully padded to conceal them. If he were searched....

He walked directly to the main doors where one of the police, the gold oak-leaf of a major on his shoulder, stood on braced legs.

"Dispatches for Governor Whiting," Wentworth told him steadily.

The eyes of the major of police were shrewd and there was a brazen egoism in the set of his lips. "Nobody goes in," he said curtly. "Governor's orders."

Wentworth frowned, then shrugged. "These were for immediate delivery," he said, indicating the dispatch case. "I flew here from New York in twenty minutes to get them in his hands, but if you want to take the responsibility, it's all right with me." He turned carelessly away.

The police major let him reach the bottom of the steps before he called Wentworth back. "I'll call the governor's secretary," he conceded.

"I'm not giving these papers to anybody except the governor," Wentworth told him flatly, but he waited while a policeman hurried away through the echoing corridors to return presently with a small dapper man who dry-washed his hands obsequiously before Wentworth.

"I'll be glad to take charge of the dispatches," he said, in a faint, disinterested voice, "and turn them over to Governor Whiting as soon as he leaves the Senate Chamber. I'm Glass, the Governor's secretary."

Wentworth frowned at the man's fawning manner, the wincing weakness of his small face. This was the sort of official chosen by the puppet masters of the state!

"Sorry," Wentworth said curtly. "My orders were to place these directly in the governor's hands—and at once. I've delivered the message. The rest is up to you."

The secretary sighed and turned away, murmuring something about "seeing the governor." The doors once more were closed and the major resumed his guardian stance before them.

"No skin off my nose now," he said.

Wentworth turned away. "I'll be at the Stadtler if I'm wanted," he said over his shoulder. None of his disappointment showed in his manner. Every minute of delay meant that so many fewer people would be listening when he began his radio broadcast. Added to that was the danger of being detected too soon since now he would be compelled to force his way into the building.

As he strolled toward the hotel, with seeming casualness, his eyes quested over the Capitol. There were many trees, growing barren with the onset of autumn, near the end of the building in which the Senate was meeting. There were also gable windows in the roof....

Wentworth smiled slightly, and his pace quickened. He entered the hotel, walked rapidly to a side door and out. He was conscious of an increasing tension within him and well he recognized the sign. To a man who lived in constant danger, as must necessarily be true for the Spider, it could mean only one thing. He was followed.

Outside the hotel door, he paused for an instant to light a cigarette. The polished platinum side of his lighter made an excellent mirror and in it he saw one of the Black Police stride up to the registry desk! Strange that they should so quickly take his trail, unless all the governor's dispatch-bearers were known—or unless Wentworth had been recognized! A dozen quick strides took Wentworth to the car he had rented. He laid the dispatch case on the seat beside him, hurled the car forward. His plans had already taken complete form. He whirled the sedan in a tight U-turn and sped back toward the Capitol grounds. The grade was sharp, but the light machine gathered speed rapidly.

A single glance sufficed to spot the tree Wentworth had selected for his daring entry into the state building—a drooping elm with a crotch not too far from the ground. A shout rang out behind him, then a police whistle laid its shrill hysteria across the night! Down the steps of the Capitol, a dozen black-clad police poured in extended order. Guns glinted in their fists. Wentworth's lips were parted in silent laughter. He wrenched over the steering-wheel, hurdled the curb and sent the sedan charging straight for the police!

A gun crashed from the head of the steps. Wentworth did not hear the lead strike, but instantly other police opened fire. Wentworth steered carefully to the right of the tree he had chosen. He caught up the briefcase and, as the car rushed on—its headlight dazzle full in the eyes of the police—he flung himself out in the shelter of the tall elm.

The guns made a furious racket in the quiet night, but the fire was all concentrated on the wildly racing car—and all eyes would be on it, too. Without an instant's delay, Wentworth sprang upward and lodged the dispatch case in the tree's fork. With that as a hand-hold, he drew himself up the thick trunk.

When the sedan struck the Capitol steps with a splintering

crash, Wentworth was already twenty feet above the ground and scrambling rapidly up the branch that arched out over the building's roof. The sedan charged half up the broad steps of the Capitol before its wheels wrenched about and sent it skittering across them. A wheel struck a column and the car reared like a stunting motorcycle, then somersaulted to a shuddering halt. The police charged in with flaming guns. Under cover of the confusion, Wentworth dangled by his hands and dropped lightly to the roof. An instant later, he had driven a foot through one of the gable windows and was in the dusty, airless attic of the Capitol itself!

Wentworth straightened with a small, triumphant smile on his lips, adjusted his clothing and threw the narrow beam of a special pocket flashlight about him, spotted a door. He was within ten feet of it when the door was flung wide open and two of the Black Police confronted him, guns in hand!

CHAPTER 4
GOVERNOR DEATH!

WENTWORTH HAD not more than a half second's warning of that door's opening. In that time he could have whipped out both automatics and been ready to blast when his enemies came in sight. The advantage was his. The flashlight had accustomed his eyes to light, and the two police were gazing into a half-dark room, themselves strongly silhouetted. It was not the fact that they were police which held the Spider in check this time. He had made his own judgment of the Black

39

Police. No doubt that they were wholly enlisted from the Under-world, or that they were ready to kill and rob on order. It was a far simpler reason that caused Wentworth to fling both hands high and call out his surrender.

He didn't want to betray his whereabouts to any more of the Black Police—and gun shots would bring them running!

Wentworth put a smile on his lips and walked toward the two police.

"You boys were smart to spot my hideout," he said equably, "but my orders are to get to the governor quickly, and I've got to do it!"

Wentworth was clear of the threshold now and already he had made his estimate of the chances. The hallway was narrow, consisting merely of a small platform at the head of a flight of iron steps which doubled on itself to the corridor of the floor below. Behind the policemen was only this flight of steps and the low railing that guarded the stair-well. Overhead, there was a single, glaring light.

"Take me to the governor."

The gun hands of the policemen relaxed a little. "Hell, if that's all it is," one said to the other, "why in hell make all this fuss about it?"

"I can't answer that one," Wentworth smiled. "They wouldn't let me see the governor, and I have to do it."

The first policeman half-turned to the other. "What do you think, Joe?" His gun sagged to his side.

Joe never answered, for this was the chance Wentworth had awaited. He seized it without a moment's preliminary bracing to betray his purpose. He hurled himself straight at the two men. His shoulder rammed into the chest of the man called Joe. The dispatch case, swung at shoulder height with the full sweep of his arm, slammed in under the chin of the second man and its metal-reinforced edge struck squarely on the larynx. He took a stumbling step backward. His hands plucked futilely at his throat, his face purpling. His larynx was paralyzed, crushed. The steps were just behind him. His body made a long arc and crumpled on the platform.

The man called Joe let out a single harsh oath as Wentworth's shoulder drove into his chest. He reeled off-balance, and the Spider checked his rush and struck a blow as solid as an ax biting into oak. The low railing caught Joe's thighs and he toppled backward, stiffly as a tree falling. His legs pointed straight up. The crunching violence of his landing on the steps, fifteen feet below, made the steel sound a deep, ringing note. Afterward, there was utter silence in the hallway.

Wentworth stood, motionless, his chest lifting a little more quickly with excitement.

No sound of alarm within the building; only the distant outdoor uproar of the police around the car.

Wentworth ran lightly down the steps. It was death he had dealt in this sharp struggle, and he paused beside the body on the platform, fingered out his platinum cigarette lighter. For an instant he hesitated in a grim weighing of perils—then he shrugged and stooped over the dead man. He thumbed open the base of the lighter, ground it down on the paling flesh of the dead policeman's forehead. When he removed it, there was a glittering vermilion insignia upon his prey, a figure of sprawling hairy legs and poison fangs—*the seal of the Spider!* Once more, beside the other policeman, Wentworth paused to imprint his seal—then hurried on.

Wentworth admitted, as he sped down the steps, that he had taken a major risk in thus branding the dead men as the Spider's victims. If he had been recognized in his own identity… He shook his head. Justice was gone from the state. If ever he were hauled before a court, accused as the Spider, the verdict would be death regardless of proof. It was well to warn the Black Police and their masters that there was a justice which still could reach them—the justice of the Spider!

More immediate perils harassed him now. Had the two men who accosted him, seen his ascent of the tree—or had they been sent by a superior? If the latter were true, there would soon be an investigation! Before then, he must be well hidden. Useless now to hope for an interview with Governor Whiting unless the Spider stole upon him in the night. But the Senate was in session….

WENTWORTH KNEW his way about the building thoroughly from the days when Stanley Kirkpatrick had been governor. He went directly to the locked doors of the Senate gallery and, from a leather girdle about his waist, slipped out a lock pick made of surgical steel. In a matter of seconds, he was inside. He locked the door behind him, and moved on soft feet across the darkened gallery until he could peer down upon the brightly lighted pit of the Senate floor itself!

Immediately, he spotted Governor Whiting's leonine head.

The state's chief executive stood beside the president's rostrum and read from a paper before him. Wentworth's lips twisted in a grim smile. He opened the big dispatch case and, in a few moments, rigged the super-sensitive microphone he had brought. It was only necessary for him to whisper into it.

"Ladies and gentlemen, citizens of New York State," he said, "I bring you the speech of Governor Whiting delivered before a secret session of the State Senate tonight. Your state is in the hands of criminals. Governor Whiting is their tool. Listen to him…."

He aimed the microphone, with its telescopic focusing tube, like a long gun—and Governor Whiting was obliging. He thundered out his speech.

"You have already given me two powerful weapons, gentlemen," said the governor. "The new system of immediate and forcible collection of taxes will fill our coffers. The New York Bureau of Investigation, with its plenipotentiary uniformed force, will insure obedience from stubborn local authorities. They have already given proof of that!"

He paused, and there was general laughter among the legislators. Plainly, there had been some incident during the day in which the Black Police had proved themselves—for their criminal masters! Wentworth was surprised and infuriated at the openness of the tyranny expressed. He had expected the usual hypocrisy—that he would have to interpolate explanations to the radio audience. But it was apparent Governor Whiting considered himself too powerful to require such subterfuge. Heaven knew what he said required no interpretation.

"Gentlemen," he was resuming, "I ask you for one more weapon. It has excellent precedent and harks back to dear old England—to our own frontier days. It has proved its efficacy against lawless elements—and against enemies of the government." Once more laughter interrupted his speech, but Whiting pressed on, lifting his voice. "I say it has proved its value too well to require much debate. I want you to vest in me the power to declare conspicuous criminals to be public enemies."

He explained.

"That is our own more modern term. In olden times, they had another name for them—outlaws."

Now he laughed. "I do not think the terminology need trouble us, but in New York state, the phrase 'public enemy' will have a special significance. If the governor proclaims that a man is a public enemy, it will immediately deprive the man of all civil rights, including the right to own property. A ten-thousand-dollar reward will be posted for him, dead or alive, and no questions asked if he is brought in dead!"

He went on. "There is one other little thing this new law will provide. In olden times, the crown immediately confiscated all the property of an outlaw. I'm afraid our constitution won't permit that, but we can do this. When a man is declared a public enemy, his property will be seized and placed in escrow pending capture. If he's brought in dead…."

Fury swept over Wentworth at the full realization of the

thing that was proposed. Its villainy was so obvious, and it was plain that the legislature would do immediately what the governor requested. It would be a terrific weapon in criminal hands. If any man lifted his hand against the authorities, or dared to protest against injustice, he would be outlawed and all his property seized. There would be scores of bounty hunters on his trail at once for his body would immediately become worth ten thousand dollars—and no questions asked! Governor Whiting already was reeling off a glib explanation for the confiscation.

"Obviously, it is a criminal's ill-gotten wealth which permits him to checkmate the law," he said. "We take that weapon away from him as we would deprive him of a knife or a gun!"

WENTWORTH STRAIGHTENED slowly where he crouched behind the railing. He had come here tonight to broadcast the infamy of officials, it was true, but he had another deeper, and more perilous, purpose. He wanted to offer himself as bait with the intention of forcing into the open whoever was behind Governor Whiting. The very idea Whiting voiced now was much too clever to have sprung from his own brain. Wentworth focused the microphone to pick up his own voice, sprang upon the balustrade and shouted his challenge!

"Governor Whiting," he cried, "you are a traitor to the state and to the people who elected you! You and these whipped curs chosen to represent the people—every one of you is in the pay of criminals! You are turning the state government into a racket, into a plaything for gangsters and killers!"

Wentworth's thundered words cut short the governor's speech. Whiting's pale face turned up toward the gallery, but there was no challenge in the lift of his leonine head—only amazement and fear.

"This is my warning to you!" Wentworth cried, his voice deep and ringing. "Criminals always fail. You will be destroyed with all your hireling thugs and killers and the master who rules you—destroyed by the people you have betrayed!"

The doors of the Senate chamber whipped open and several of the black-clad police darted in. Governor Whiting lifted a long arm and leveled it at Wentworth like a gun.

"Kill that man!" he screamed.

A score more of the Black Police jammed into the doorways. In moments, too, they would be at the doors of the gallery. Wentworth laughed and dropped behind the balustrade an instant before the guns crashed out. But he was not through. While he drew two tear-gas bombs from the dispatch case, and lobbed them down into the pit of the Senate Chamber, he was talking rapidly into the microphone.

"You have heard the governor's message," he said, "and the danger to every citizen in his plan is too clear for me to have to explain. You heard the governor order me killed when I challenged him, and you can hear the guns as the criminal Black Police try to carry out his orders. I must go now before they succeed! But think well on what you have heard. When the call comes, be ready to act." He paused, and then threw his laughter into the microphone, the flat mocking laughter of the Spider. He whispered, *"The Spider has spoken!"*

FROM THE dispatch case, Wentworth took out a silk, goggled mask and crouched, waiting, until the blasting of the guns gave way to panic shouts and strangling coughs with the spreading of the gas. There was a pounding at the gallery doors now. Wentworth lifted his head, cautiously. The legislators were streaming toward the exits, carrying the police before them as they fled from the torture of the tear-gas.

Wentworth slipped on the mask, left the radio equipment and climbed over the railing. The drop was not too high. Moments later, he fled from the Senate Chamber among a dozen coughing, terrified men. Their flight had swept away all the guards. Wentworth whipped off the mask, coughed rackingly.

"Whoever did that," he gasped to his nearest neighbor, "ought to be hung now!"

It was easy then to detach himself from the stampede and make his way presently to the office of Governor Whiting in the building. It was deserted, locked, but doors offered no barriers to the skill of the Spider. Presently Wentworth was gazing, narrow-eyed, at a concave mirror set into the wall of Whiting's private office. It exactly matched that mirror which had vomited machine-gun death in the Ducamps Building. What secret this one hid he did not know, but he thought that presently Governor Whiting would solve that for him!

The private office boasted a fireplace in which a grate of channel coals threw out grateful warmth. Wentworth settled himself before it in a wing-chair, poured a drink, softly turned on the radio at his right hand. He forced himself to relax. It required all Wentworth's will-power to effect this because of the anger that burned through his veins. As Kirkpatrick had charged, Wentworth had been merely guessing about a criminal overlord for governor and legislature. The things he had heard this night had gone far beyond even his fears.

It was plain that the people no longer could look to the government of the state for protection. Henceforth, they were victims to be robbed of whatever wealth they possessed, maltreated by the police; ruthlessly slaughtered, and legally— through this new outlaw-proclamation system—if they so much as dared to protest. And this gang was being careful to allow no loophole by which the Federal officials could step into the picture. Criminal law, with certain notable exceptions, was a matter for state enforcement. So long as they fought clear of any Federal-protected organization, they were safe on that score.

Wentworth swore under his breath, moved restlessly in the chair. He would force some truth from Whiting, if he had to kidnap the man and torture him! Public officials who betrayed their trust deserved no mercy—and would receive none from the Spider!

His attention swung sharply toward the radio over which now came the voice of a news commentator.

"Mayor Culkin, of New York City, tonight declared that the police department had mutinied against his authority," the man said rapidly. "He charged that the commissioner, Stanley Kirkpatrick, had refused to accept his orders and was leading a small squad of men in resistance to state officials who were attempting to collect the new tax voted at Albany today. According to the mayor, Kirkpatrick refused to give any explanation of his actions and other men, loyal to him, have barricaded police headquarters against the mayor and other city officials. Mayor Culkin threatened to ask Governor Whiting to dispatch companies of the National Guard, unless Kirkpatrick surrendered his office within the hour."

A slight bitter smile moved Wentworth's lips. He needed no more details to guess what really had happened. Some of the thugs of the Black Police had invaded New York City and attempted to enforce their racketeering tax as they had in Poughkeepsie. Kirkpatrick, with his stern sense of justice, had gone to battle for the people. It was a gallant gesture, but a foolish one. Kirkpatrick was finished now. Certainly, he would not fight the National Guard, though the veteran police were well able to hold their own against civilian soldiery. Much wiser to have dissembled, bided his time. But Kirkpatrick was incapable of such deceptions. Wentworth's heart contracted with fear for his friend. If only he could reach him, warn him....

Wentworth's hand snapped to the radio and clicked it into silence. He thrust himself more deeply into the shadows of the chair which was large enough to conceal him entirely in the half-light. He had heard the metallic rasp of a key in the outer door. Even as he settled himself, Governor Whiting fairly ran into the inner office. He closed and locked the door.

A THIN smile brushed Wentworth's lips. He slid an automatic from its holster—and then sat rigidly still. For Whiting did not

49

even wait to turn on the lights. He ran directly to the mirror set in the wall, took his stand immediately before it. His voice came out, huskily, anxious.

"White face in the mirror," he whispered. "White face in the mirror."

Wentworth slid quietly from the chair and, crouching in its shadow, watched the governor. Even in the half-light from the fire, it was plain that Whiting was trembling. He mopped his forehead, repeated the phrase again. Then Wentworth smothered a curse, for in the heart of the mirror—lights began to glow, lights that gradually took form and became... *a white face!* Its lips moved and a deep, solemn voice spoke from the mirror!

"Why do you summon me?" it demanded.

Governor Whiting babbled out the happenings in the Senate chamber. Wentworth's narrowed gaze concentrated on that face in the mirror. Quite obviously, it was a creation of lights in that concave surface. Some such sonic-operated device as had, in Ducamps office, discharged the machine gun, could be employed. But Wentworth had a sharp certainty that this was a man's actual face upon which he was gazing. If not the face itself, then a reflection of a man's face worked by some sort of *camera obscura*. His gun lifted slowly in his hand. The voice in the mirror was speaking again....

"The man in the Senate chamber," it said, "was Richard Wentworth, the friend of Stanley Kirkpatrick. He broadcast your speech on outlawry, by short-wave radio. Outlaw both Wentworth and Kirkpatrick. Hurry those pardons to the prisons."

Governor Whiting stammered, "Yes, yes, of course."

Wentworth's lips parted in soundless laughter. In a long bound, he reached Whiting's side. His gun barrel flicked against the governor's head, drove him unconscious to the floor. In the next instant, Wentworth smashed the mirror to fragments. He flung the beam of his flashlight into the recess it revealed—*not* a recess, but a narrow corridor!

A cry of triumph sprang softly from Wentworth's lips. In an instant, he was clambering into the secret corridor he had revealed; which he had guessed must be there. If that face could answer a direct question, which could not have been anticipated, then it was the voice of an actual man. And that man must be somewhere along this corridor!

His questing light revealed a narrow, twisting flight of steps that led downward and Wentworth bounded to them, sped light-footedly on his quest. Governor Whiting would remain unconscious for a half hour or more. He was locked in his office, and outside interference was unlikely. The Spider's back was protected and ahead, somewhere, was the key to the mystery, to the criminal who held in his greedy hands the reins of the state government!

The spiral of steps was steep and led straight down, without a side opening, for a full thirty feet. Abruptly, Wentworth seized the railing and jerked himself to a halt—but not quite in time. He turned his shoulder and caught his weight as he ran full-tilt into a brick wall! Wentworth stared in amazement, flung the beam of his light upward. He was in a narrow well, precisely the size of the stairway, and its end was a blank wall!

Plainly, there was some secret doorway on the stairs, either here at its base or somewhere along its thirty-foot length. Wentworth tapped sharply on the bricks with the muzzle of his automatic, but the sound was solid as earth itself. Probably the hidden exit was somewhere above. A soft, metallic sound over his head jerked Wentworth's head upward, and a harsh curse sprang to his lips. A steel grating had slid into place. He was a prisoner here in the bottom of the shaft!

Even as Wentworth's eyes took in that fact, he became aware of another thing. His lips were dry and there was odd heat in his blood. He felt as if he were burning up with fever! He clapped a hand on the railing of the stairway and it was cold to his touch. The walls were cold, too. He laid his forehead against the bricks. His lips were parted and his breath was coming more rapidly.

For the first time then, he knew a touch of fear. Fever in his blood… God, he knew the answer to that! Science had devised a way of inducing artificial fever by means of ultra-short wave currents of electricity. He was in the focus of such a machine. Already weakness was coursing through him. His brain felt swollen, light. A few minutes more and he would be delirious, and after that… after that, death!

CHAPTER 5
TAXES AND TERROR

IN WENTWORTH'S New York home, Nita van Sloan paced the long third-floor drawing-room with worry in her violet eyes. She had heard Dick's broadcast from the legislature, heard his voice fade out amid the crashing of hostile guns. Yet that alone should not bring her such terror. Dick had fought his way through a hundred gun battles without serious harm. But terror walked with her, nonetheless.

From the refugees Wentworth had sent to her, she had heard the story of the fight in Poughkeepsie. It was like Dick to send Jack Wilson and the old priest, Tony Manteo and Angela, to his own home for protection, but it was also a dangerous thing. It would give the police an excuse to smash their way in, if they learned of the presence of the four. And it added little to the strength of the fortress—even if Jack Wilson walked the guard rounds with Ram Singh.

Nita's thoughts were harassed. She could not help but feel that there was some salient point in the situation which she should have grasped, and yet missed. She sent her mind questing over the developments of the night. The newspapers and radio commentators had been strangely silent on events in New York State. There was a bare mention of the emergency tax, of the new police force created "because of the breakdown in local enforcement." Then had come Dick's startling broadcast, and the governor's demand for power to issue outlawry proclamations. No doubt that his request would be granted by the subservient legislature... Nita stopped her pacing abruptly. Dick had told her that he intended to allow himself to be identified, to bait the real leader of the criminals into the open!

Surely, the next step was obvious. Wentworth would be outlawed, his property confiscated! Heavens! The order might already have been issued! Could she defend the mansion against the police? It might be possible with the powerful armament

Wentworth had devised and with the proper garrison of men. But what would that accomplish? In the end, the fortress would be forced....

Ram Singh glided into the doorway.

"Kirkpatrick *sahib* asks for you, *missie sahib.*" Ram Singh cupped his hands to his forehead in a salaam only a little less reverent than that he gave his master. He had fought under Nita's orders, too, and knew her power and her strength.

Nita crossed rapidly to a phone and caught it up. "No, Stanley," she said presently, "I haven't heard from Dick. The broadcast? But that was the Spider—didn't you hear?"

Kirkpatrick's voice came to her with restrained urgency. "If he calls you, Nita, for God's sake have him get in touch with me at once! Tell him I'll be fortunate if I can hold out one more day as commissioner. Tell him I'll fight beside him from now on! The things that have happened tonight are damnable. The Black Police have moved into New York. I saw a woman flogged because she resisted the taxes. A man was hanged in his shop."

Nita drew in her breath, shakily, "I'll tell Dick—if he calls," she said.

THE CITY THAT PAID TO DIE

NITA VAN SLOAN

"Do that." Kirkpatrick hesitated a moment longer. "I... I need his help."

Nita was more shaken than she dared admit to herself when she hung up the phone. When Kirkpatrick called on the Spider for help—when a man to whom duty and the law were sacred, volunteered to follow the Spider—things must indeed be desperate. But even while Nita had talked to him, a resolution was taking form in her mind. If Dick was to be outlawed, and she had no doubt of that, only one course was open to her. She must gather such weapons as she could, assemble all his available cash, and flee to some hiding place until such time as she could unite with Dick, himself. Already, the house might be under surveillance....

Nita struck her hands sharply together, and Ram Singh was instantly in the doorway. Nita beckoned the faithful Sikh toward her, swiftly outlined her fears and their plan of action.

"Only this remains," she finished. "Where can we hide? The *sahib* has places to which he, himself, can retreat, but we have others to protect. It must be somewhere we can find weapons and wealth."

Ram Singh's eyes held a fierce light. There are countrymen of mine who will serve until death!" he cried.

Nita shook her head. "They would be immediately suspected because of you. Think further, Ram Singh." Abruptly she turned toward him. "Chei Hwang-yo!" she cried softly. "The *sahib* did him a great service once. He slew the monster who was taking Chinatown away from Chei Hwang-yo and destroying it. Do you know how to reach him?"

Ram Singh's teeth flashed white through his thick beard. "There is a way, from the river," he said.

NITA RAPIDLY laid her plans, and called every person in the house, except the injured Tony Manteo, into service. Weapons were carried in staggering loads to the library on the first floor. This entire room actually was an elevator that would drop them to the level of the secret hangar and boathouse underneath the piers between which the house was built. The aged butler, Jenkyns, who had served Wentworth's father before him, was bewildered at the threatened change, but adjusted himself quickly. When Nita had loaded the last of the weapons into the room, he was busy preparing a midnight lunch for them.

Nita issued her orders to them then. "Jenkyns will operate the elevator," she said. "Load all this equipment in the motorboat he will show you. Keep this door locked regardless of what happens. Mr. Wilson, you will be in command. I'll be back within a half, or three-quarters of an hour. You must be sure to be ready then."

Outside the door, she faced Ram Singh, resolutely. "The *sahib* keeps a hundred thousand dollars in cash in each of two safety-deposit boxes, on opposite sides of the city, for emergencies like this. I have access, and we must get it. The cash that he keeps on hand here will not suffice if there is a long siege. Get out the Daimler. See that the automatics and machine guns are ready for immediate use. And, Ram Singh—*hurry!*"

Once inside the bullet-proof car, and hurrying toward the all-night safety-deposit box vaults, Nita felt less frightened. If she were wrong in her expectations—if Wentworth were not outlawed—no harm had been done. But she had no doubts, really. There was another fear at the back of her mind which she dared not admit even to herself. All of this was futile, useless, if anything had happened to Dick!

There was no trouble at either of the banks. Three times, patrols of Black Police crossed their path, but Ram Singh swung wide about them. Once Nita heard a woman screaming, terribly, and she clutched the sub-machine gun across her lap while her heart contracted. But she could not help there. It was so much more important for Dick to have the means to fight against these tyrants. He would smash them, if only… Nita resolutely closed her mind on the thought of harm befalling Dick. She thought, instead, of his strength and his keen brain and the unfailing accuracy of his guns. If she could have known that at this very moment Wentworth lay, half-fainting, a prisoner at the bottom of that hellish well!

Ram Singh's abrupt application of brakes pulled her forward on the seat, both hands clutching the gun across her lap.

"What is it?" she cried softly, but even as she spoke, she saw the reason he had halted. A motorcycle crawled past the cross-street with its siren shrilling and one of the Black Police in the saddle. Immediately behind it was another, and another, and Nita heard a cry that soared even above the moan of the sirens—a man's scream!

Ram Singh cut off the lights, let the car drift to the curb and they remained there like that while a slow procession filed across the end of the street. Immediately behind the siren-shrieking police rolled a truck. Nita's breath caught in her throat, as she saw that three men were lashed to the tail-gate by their wrists.

Behind them walked two of the Black Police with heavy whips. At regular intervals, one of them swung the lash viciously across the naked backs of the men!

Along the side of the truck ran a sign on which crude red letters had been painted. It read—*They Didn't Pay the Poor Tax.*

That truck was only the first of the procession, and the screams that came to Nita's ears now were women's voices! Her hand flew to the catch of the door, the gun ready across her lap—then she checked. What could she possibly accomplish? There wasn't a chance that, charging that line of police, she could free those poor victims. Nita cried out, herself, as the third truck in that cruel line rolled past. The whip man whirled his lash high and brought it down across the naked back of a woman. With a scream of utter agony, she sagged in her lashings. The truck did not stop, though the woman dangled by her lashed wrists, half her beaten body dragging on the paved street!

Nita heard curses rumble from Ram Singh's throat. If she but spoke the word… Abruptly, a motorcycle whirled into the street and rushed toward them!

Nita's voice came out harshly. "Is your knife ready, Ram Singh?" she asked coldly.

Ram Singh laughed sharply once, an explosive sound. The motorcycle slued to a halt beside them, and the policeman had his gun in his hand—a Black policeman with the face of a killer, of a criminal, beneath his visor.

"We need this car!" he shouted. "Swing into line. Swing in, damn you, or somebody else will drive, and you'll walk behind, under the whip."

RAM SINGH slowly cranked down the window and looked at the officer through a long moment. He said, quite clearly. "Pig!" At the same instant, his hand whipped over. There was a minute gleam of silvery steel, then the policeman pitched backward into the street, kicking, plucking at the hilt that protruded from his throat.

Nita swallowed. "An excellent throw, Ram Singh," she said flatly.

The Sikh slid to the pavement and regained his knife. His teeth showed white through his beard as he moved back again. *"Wah, missie sahib,"* he said, his deep voice rumbling, "these are not men. They are snakes and their heads are easily crushed."

Nita's anger burst out ringingly. "We'll crush a few snakes, Ram Singh!" she cried.

The end of the procession was passing the street corner now. She made a swift estimate of the number of police in the procession... Not more than twenty. She leaned forward and unhooked a second machine gun from the rack, held it out to Ram Singh. Nita's was a woman's heart, and merciful. She had always deplored the lives that had sped at Wentworth's hands. But anger was on her now—anger at injustice, the strong, implacable fury which she had glimpsed on Wentworth's face... and trembled to see. But these were not men. They were beasts of prey!

"Quickly, Ram Singh," she ordered, "before they miss their

fellow-snake. Roll up the right-hand side of the street past the procession. There are three trucks besides the motorcycles in front. I'll take the first truck. Be sure you don't kill the drivers. Wound them so that they'll have to stop the trucks."

Ram Singh threw back his head and laughed, "*Wah!*" he cried. "Thou art one worthy to be the mate of the *sahib!*"

The great car lunged forward. Nita leaned forward and opened a narrow port in the left-hand window. The machine gun rested on her lap. In her right hand was an automatic pistol. She was glad that Wentworth had taught her how to shoot!

The Daimler rounded the corner and rolled toward the last of the trucks. The two whip men paid no attention until too late. They were too intent on torturing their victims. As the brute of a man nearest her lifted the whip again to lay it across cut and bleeding flesh, Nita drew a careful bead and squeezed the trigger. The gun sound inside of the closed limousine was terribly loud, but she knew its blast would not carry far outside. The truck engines were too noisy.

The man she had shot lurched sideways, almost tripped his companion. The second flogger twisted about a white, amazed face. He clawed for his gun. Nita waited for a long moment, her gun level and ready. When he had his hand on the butt of his revolver, she fired again. It was only when Nita had her automatic ready to fire at the truck's driver that she realized the mistake she had made. She could not shoot him lest the lunging truck crush those poor helpless women tied to the tail of the machine ahead. She should have struck the leading truck first. It was too late now!

Even as Nita hesitated, Ram Singh opened fire on the police around the truck ahead. Nita had waited too long. The truck driver saw her and, in desperation, whirled the heavy truck straight toward the creeping Daimler! The crash hurled Nita to the floor. Her head struck the door frame, leaving her dazed. Through a fog of whirling blackness, she heard the crash of guns. She forced herself upward, just in time. A gun muzzle was thrust into the gun port she had opened!

Nita's automatic spoke almost before she was aware of aiming. The muzzle vanished from the port, and a man's scream soared horribly. Then Nita was on her knees, peering out at the scene. The truck ahead had been jammed across the street to block any possible escape. From its cover, bullets rained on the bullet-proof glass, the armored sides of the Daimler. Already the windshield was frosted over so that it was almost impossible to see through it. How could it withstand this pounding of the bullets of the Black Police!

Ram Singh's sub-machine gun was stammering in short, vicious bursts and already a half dozen uniformed bodies spotted the street.

"Can you back the car?" Nita asked, quietly. "I'll hold them in check."

Ram Singh shook his head, "I am a fool, *missie sahib,*" he said. "I allowed them to wreck the steering gear. I allowed you to make this attack, and the master put thy life into my hands! They shall not have thee while I live, *missie sahib!*"

A section of the windshield crumpled and thudded to the floor, and the triumphant shouts of the police reached Nita's ears. She twisted her head about. She could see the men at the rear of the truck, the prisoners. They were crouching low under the tail to keep clear of bullets, but she could see their wrists and the rope that bound them—a single rope that stretched from side to side. Nita laughed softly. Poor reinforcements, but better than none!

She drew careful bead with her automatic and fired. Three shots were necessary before the rope was severed.

"To me!" she called clearly then. "I have guns for you!"

A man's head lifted slowly above the tail-gate. His face was drawn with suffering, but there was a hard set to the jaw. He tugged at the severed rope, freed his hands. Nita opened the window beside her more widely and tossed a fully loaded automatic to the man. He ducked out of sight again and, presently, she heard the automatic blast out. She saw one of the skulking police throw up his hands and pitch to the pavement, and Nita *laughed!*

She armed the other two men. "Get in the truck!" she called. "Back it away and charge them!"

AS IF the police sensed the turn in the tide of battle, they launched a furious charge. Ram Singh shouted his challenge, and the sub-machine gun swung a crisp deadly arc. Nita's own weapon was sputtering now. She scarcely noticed when the truck wrenched away from the car, but she saw it loom across her sights and released the trigger.

With the cessation of her fire, a great ringing stillness descended on the streets. Her ears ached with it and, through a long moment, it puzzled her. Then she realized that the police who remained have had fled! She had won!

Dimly, a siren began to sound. Its shriek swelled rapidly.

"Quickly, Ram Singh!" she cried. "We'll take one of those motorcycles! Tell those men in the truck to free the others and to drive to Chatham Square. If we win through, we'll care for them! They'll make allies in this battle!"

Minutes later, with the sirens almost upon them, the truck load of tortured creatures rumbled off down a side street. Ram Singh wheeled over a motorcycle and Nita mounted the saddle with the Sikh clinging behind her. The machine gathered speed, swept without lights eastward toward the fortress mansion.

As long as she was dodging the police, excitement held Nita up, but the reaction set in swiftly once the steel gates of the fortress clanged behind her. Her mouth corners twitched and there was a coldness through all her body. She had killed....

"Quickly," she gasped to Ram Singh, "to the boat. They'll identify the limousine."

She stumbled through the hallway toward the library, used her key. The last of the weapons had been cleared away. She thrust the money into Ram Singh's hands. "To the boat," she ordered, panting. "I must get off a radio message to Jackson, if I can—to warn the *sahib* in time."

Ram Singh bowed, and Nita whipped open the door of a closet in the hall, released a secret panel there and began to pound out a message on the wireless key. She must hint, rather than tell where they were going, and hope that Dick would understand. Too many could hear the wireless—for her to risk the truth….

Swiftly her wrist bobbed with the movements of the key. Swiftly… almost in her ear, the gun crashed out. The sending set was smashed by the bullet. She spun around, realizing that she had thrown aside her weapon in the library; realizing, too, that she was alone in the house. The others were all aboard the boat, waiting for her.

She turned, and looked into the muzzle of a revolver held by one of the Black Police. His grin was wolfish, cruel.

"Well have to work out something new to punish you," he said. "Death, of course, in the end…."

CHAPTER 6
FUGITIVE FROM FURY

AND IN Albany, imprisoned in the well, Wentworth battled frantically against the fever in his brain, trying to force coherent thought. All his senses felt deadened. His ears rang. He had been staring at the grill which, closing off the stairs above him, held him captive. For several long moments, in the thin light of his flash, he had actually seemed to see the gleaming metal bars. If he could move those….

The idea was preposterous and yet Wentworth moved up toward the grill, clinging to the railing, draining his flagging strength to reach the bars. He reached up a tentative hand, while his eyes ran along the grill toward the brick wall from which the steel spikes thrust out separately. And he didn't touch the bars.

Something stopped him, and it was other long moments before he realized the truth. Dimly, then, he knew that each of the rods was insulated from the bricks through which they passed. That meant they carried electricity....

Foggily, the idea penetrated to his dulled brain. Somewhere in this newfound knowledge was a solution, if only he could arrive at it. It still seemed to him that his body had an independent intelligence—that it went about tasks before his brain knew why. His hands moved with a fumbling slowness that was torture. Everything depended on speed. He knew that. He ripped off a shoe and, using the lace, he bound one of his automatics at right angle across the toe. Leather would not conduct electricity—not so well as his gun.

It seemed to take hours to stretch out his arm, gripping the heel of the shoe. He knew now what he intended to do. He would form a solid contact between the grilling and the wall, using the automatic to short-circuit the hookup that was draining him of strength and killing him. The wall seemed to drift away from his out-reaching hand. He was leaning far out over the railing....

Blinding, blue-white flame seemed to strike him in the face. Wentworth felt himself hurled backward but managed to bow his head and protect it from concussion. The flashlight was gone from his hand, but he had no need of it. The sputter of electric fire still filled the well with eerie light and the fresh, energizing odor of ozone stung his nostrils. The arcing of the current had welded the automatic's muzzle against the steel bar, held the butt rigidly against the wall. The bar was glowing red hot at the point of contact—and the fever was gone from him.

With a violent effort, he forced himself erect. Hot steel could be bent! His brain was clearing, though a numb weakness still gripped him. He inspected the bar, then, fumbling, removed his coat, slipped a sleeve over the bar and threw all his weight upon it. The odor of scorching cloth closed his nostrils, strangled him—but the bar yielded!

A few moments of strenuous effort, and he had bent the bar sufficiently to be able to squeeze his body through. He fought his way weakly up the stairs, dragging his coat, one shoe missing. His face still wore the high flush of fever and his forehead was wet with the perspiration of weakness. The single gun he still carried seemed almost too heavy to be borne. Somewhere nearby, he knew, was the secret chamber from which these mechanisms had operated, but Wentworth was too spent to solve the problem now. Even his clothing was an intolerable burden as he fought his way up the incalculable miles of steps toward the faint light that showed overhead.

At last, he stood swaying in the opening where the governor's mirror had been. The office was empty. Either Whiting had recovered or been carried out. Everything else was exactly as before—the soft warmth of the fire, the amber glow of whisky in a decanter. Nothing out of place except for the glittering shards of mirror on the floor.

WENTWORTH TOOK a stiff drink, and it brought back some of his strength. He fought for clarity of thought. To be so close to the nub of the mystery and then to fail… His eyes swung

GOVERNOR
WHITING

GLASS

MAYOR CULKINS

to the opening in the wall, and grimness tautened his cheeks. He hefted the automatic in his fist. He felt better able to use it now. He took a single stride forward, then checked, listening.

Footsteps in the outer office, a stampede of them! That would be the Black Police hurrying to the kill!

For an instant Wentworth paused, on the brink of battle. He swore under his breath. No way of telling how many of the police were out there, but the sound of shots would bring scores more. Even so, Wentworth might have stayed to fight, if he could have hoped for any profit from the skirmish. Well he knew that, long before he could rout the killers, and search out the hiding place of the "White Face in the Mirror," the criminal—whose trap he had so narrowly escaped—would have fled.

No, his only recourse was flight. In a swift stride, Wentworth reached the window and whipped it open. On the ledge, he paused long enough to close it before he jumped to the earth a few feet below—the noise the police made covered the sound— then he was limping off into the shadows. He had again drawn on his coat with its scorched sleeve. The ground was cold beneath his shoeless foot, but the chill of the autumn night stimulated

CHEI HWANG YO

SAILOR JOE

him and his stride lengthened. The weakness of the fever was still upon him. It was his will that drove him on—his will and his furious anger at himself.

It was true that he had accomplished the two things for which he had come to Albany, but he knew now they would avail nothing. His most pessimistic imaginings had never pictured such absolute criminal control of the government as he had uncovered. True, also, he had succeeded in getting a broadcast past the control which Whiting and his underlings already had established over press and radio. Such people as had heard it must be convinced of the things he had declared. But the plain truth was that, even with that knowledge, they would be helpless. Short of armed revolt, which would destroy the governor, his legislators and the infamous Black Police, what else would suffice?

His foray undoubtedly would delay Whiting for a brief while in his plans. But it was unlikely the governor would wait for the passage of the law to hurl the full force of his "public enemy" proclamation against Wentworth and Kirkpatrick. Why, damn it, unless he moved swiftly he would be without even funds to battle against the criminals! He must get word to Nita van Sloan, to Kirkpatrick, and meantime he must evade capture. Fortunately, the city streets were nearly deserted, for he was a marked man with his one shoe and his torn coat.

GRIMLY, WENTWORTH forced himself to the decision which alone could help him in his warfare. He must turn his back on Albany where the criminal undoubtedly was for the present—must flee to New York and assemble reinforcements. Wentworth paused in a darkened recess of a store entrance and gazed back at the Capitol. In this brief while, it had been turned into a fortress.

There were sand-bag barricades at the main doors and the glint of machine guns behind it. As he watched, armored trucks rolled up. Their blazing searchlights began to play over the grounds while squads of Black Police marched and countermarched in their search for the man who had defied them! Wentworth had escaped only just in time.

God, what could one man hope to accomplish against that armed might! He had succeeded only in arming Governor Whiting and his subordinates. Yet he must reach them before he could penetrate beyond to the true identity of the White Face in the Mirror. Until the Master was destroyed, the lopping off of limbs would accomplish little. A feeling of despair flooded Wentworth. For once, he had met a combination which all the cleverness of the Spider could not conquer single-handed. Beyond any doubt, he must have reinforcements....

Wentworth glanced at his watch. It was time for Jackson to meet him at their rendezvous. Wentworth slid along, close in the shadows of dark buildings, toward the spot. Patrol trucks were beginning to roll through the streets with questing searchlights, with machine-gun armed men. Governor Whiting would make very sure that there were no hostile gatherings on his doorstep!

One thing was immediately apparent to Wentworth, as he raced on across Albany, dodging into the shadows whenever a patrol truck came near. Whiting and the Master must find recruits for their Black Police, men who would obey their orders without scruple—criminals ready to kill at a moment's notice....

"Good God!" Wentworth stopped, suddenly remembering. When Governor Whiting had stood before the White Face in the Mirror, to receive instructions for outlawing Kirkpatrick and Wentworth, there had been an additional order. The Master had said, *"Hurry those pardons to the prisons!"*

No need to wonder now about his meaning. Recruits for the Black Police would come from the prisons of the state. Hard-ened criminals who would go through hell for their liberators, under the threat of return to narrow cells—and the promise of rich loot! The curse that rose to Wentworth's lips was almost a sob. He broke into a sloping run, checked suddenly to the sound of guns. It came from straight ahead—from the spot of the rendezvous!

Wentworth gripped his automatic and plunged forward again, whirled a corner, then flung himself prone. His fears were too well justified. The radio truck which Jackson had oper-ated was wrecked against an apartment building. From behind the armored sides of a truck, a half dozen men were pouring deadly fire into the car. One of the Black Police had now spotted Wentworth and his bullets scored the concrete on which he lay!

In desperation, Wentworth crawled back around the corner and put the protection of a brick wall between himself and those killers. He was in front of a low building, formerly a private home which now had a "Vacancy" sign for roomers in the window. In three strides, he had reached the door, and once more the lock pick came into play. Moments later, he was bounding up the steps toward the roof. But when he peered down into the street, it was swarming with Black Police. Three other trucks had stopped there. He saw them drag Jackson's limp body from the wrecked radio car and his automatic dropped into line of its own accord....

But the Spider did not fire. He could not battle fifty men single-handed, with any hope of success. He did not even know if the loyal Jackson still lived. Even so, Wentworth would have chanced that battle... But a graver duty called. The Spider had no right to risk his life in this purely personal affray. With what he knew and had guessed, it might be possible to form an alliance with Kirkpatrick which could weaken and then smash this oligarchy of crime.

Regretfully, Wentworth thrust the automatic into its holster and resumed once more his flight across the city. He masked his face, held up and bound the night man at a garage; took his shoes and one of the stored cars. He delayed long enough to put through a telephone call to his home in New York City. It seemed hours that he waited in the tight, smelly office of the garage, listening to the murmur along the wires. He heard the bell buzz on and on—on and on in his home.

"Your party does not answer," the operator reported.

Wentworth felt fear choking him. "There must be someone there!" he cried.

The formality of the operator's voice was maddening. "I'll ring your party again, sir."

More ringing; more silence. Wentworth swore and slammed up the receiver. In God's name what had happened to Nita! Even if she had left the house against his orders, Jenkyns should still be there... unless the Black Police already had struck!

WENTWORTH HURLED himself from the garage office like a madman. No need to speculate on what had happened in New York. Somehow, the Black Police, or other emissaries of the Master, had found their way into his home and now Nita… Wentworth realized that he had bitten through his lower lip.

Twice on his mad race across Albany, Wentworth was intercepted by flying squadrons of Black Police. They couldn't stop him. There was a frenzy on him that not even bullets would break. Each time, he fired just one shot at the pursuing cars. The first time, he killed the driver outright. The second time, he shot off a front tire. The chase ended like that. Fifteen minutes after he had slammed up the useless phone, Wentworth was on the flying field. There were police there, too. The hangar was closed and the men in black ringed it against invasion.

A semblance of sanity returned to Wentworth then—and the knowledge that no matter how soon he reached New York City, he would be too late to help Nita. But not too late to strike at the Master and his men! Kirkpatrick still remained to be saved. Afterward, there would be a reckoning. His decision was made in the same instant that he recognized the impossibility of storming the hangar.

He swung the wheel of the car over as the Black Police opened fire and jammed in behind the administration building. Another tight turn, and he was headed straight for the broad door. Wentworth braced himself rigidly against steering wheel and dashboard and the car crashed, stalled. In low gear, he pushed it on. He could hear shouts and more shouts now above the hammer of the engine, but he paid no heed. The spinning wheels gripped. There was a rending of wood and metal and the car burst through into the main hall of the building. It was the work of an instant to jump out, to fire a shot through the gasoline tank.

Two minutes later, when the charging Black Police reached the building, gasoline-fed flames were leaping high, sweeping the walls, crawling hungrily across the floor. In the luridly lit interior, Wentworth crouched behind a partition with a ready gun. He opened his lips with a scream that tore with pure agony. He kept that up for thirty seconds or more, and then the gasoline tank of the car let go.

The Black Police were milling around the collapsed door. Wentworth watched his opportunity and slipped out the opposite side. There were no guards around the hangar, naturally. These men were not disciplined forces. His lips twisted in a thin smile, he sprinted for the building where the planes were stored. He managed to enter it without being detected. A speedy sport monoplane was poised behind the doors. Wentworth started the motor before he sprang to the wide hangar doors. Fortunately, they were counter-balanced, easy to operate. A thrust sent them sliding upward, and he leaped to the wing of the monoplane, to the cockpit.

HE SET the brakes, eased the throttle gradually wider. The cold motor spluttered, faltered, roared for a moment—missed again. Through the widening arch of the door, Wentworth peered toward the burning building. The police had spotted him now all right. Several of them were sprinting toward him, guns crashing. A cold smile moved Wentworth's lips. He jockeyed the throttle even wider, then lifted his automatic. There was a thought in his brain that almost became spoken words....

"For Nita!" His lifted automatic fell implacably in line, and he squeezed the trigger. He did that three times, as deliberately as at target practice, and three men fell to the ground. The fourth turned and fled. Wentworth lined his automatic, then held his fire—not in mercy. He might need his cartridges presently.

Headlights were streaming along the road from Albany, more Black Police. They could stop him all right with a car. Cold as the spluttering motor was, he would have to risk a take-off. He eased the brakes, let the plane trundle down the ramp to the field. Police were firing on him from the cover of the administration building. A bullet snicked through the fabric close by his shoulder. Wentworth yanked the throttle wide, heard the motor choke, falter, then pick up. The plane began to roll faster, faster a car swerved wildly out on the field, endeavoring to cut across his path. With lips grimly set, Wentworth held his course true.

Gently, he tried the stick, levered the plane's tail off the ground. The automobile was dangerously close now. Guns blazed. Angrily, Wentworth leveled his automatic, fired. He had missed! No time for another shot. Savagely, Wentworth yanked back the stick, felt the sluggish lift of the ship. If the motor faltered now... Five, ten feet he gained—fifteen. Wentworth thrust the stick forward again, felt his momentum pick up. Just as the wheels were skimming the ground, headed for a certain crackup with the car, he used his increasing speed to zoom.

Men were screaming below him. He caught their voices in a brief gust of sound, then they were left behind and the plane

THE CITY THAT PAID TO DIE

was climbing in a steady long slant toward the southeast, toward New York City. He was safe now. His burning of the administration building served more than one purpose. He had destroyed telephone communication from the field. Before the police could reach another instrument and have guards sent to New York fields, he would have landed....

His landing would be safe enough, but after that... Wentworth's lips twisted bitterly. He must try to find and warn Kirkpatrick and then—prepare for battle! A coldness that had nothing to do with the bite of the upper air crept over him. He had battled before against desperate odds, but never before against a monster who ruled an entire state—where even the supposed forces of law and order fought on the side of crime!

CHAPTER 7
DISASTER!

THE LIGHTS of New York City soon lifted above the horizon, the buildings looking like a black, crowded badlands against the dirty gray of the first dawn. Soon the smokes of a thousand furnaces would blot it out, but at present the silhouette was clear and strong, a man-created beauty that never failed to stir Wentworth. It was grief that moved him now. Men could create, but men could destroy, too, and it was the destructive element that held reign over his city.

It was not often that doubt or hesitancy shook Wentworth. He had chosen the path of service long ago when shaken by a too young discovery of the injustices which dominated the

world of men. He had never regretted it for himself, but no man could live alone. He had dragged others into the maw of warfare through their affection for him. Brave Jackson, a prisoner or dead in Albany; Nita... gone. Men had died in his service before this, in the thankless task of championing people who, in the mass, would turn on him for the rewards offered for his life.

Wentworth's automatic crashed out twice, and two Black Police struck the floor!

Wentworth's firmly chiseled mouth set awry in a bitter smile. The thought was not new but it came with special poignancy in this gray dawn when, close to exhaustion and bereft, he pressed on into the battle. Despite his careful stratagems in Albany, the bullets of the Black Police might well be waiting for him at the air fields of New York. Even when he had braved them, he could not speed then to the help of those toward whom his heart yearned. His duty, self-imposed though it was, bade him speed to warn Kirkpatrick—to find fresh battles. Only afterward could he even think of Nita and Jackson.

The city was sweeping toward him, and Wentworth made his decision. Rather than risk the landing fields, he would risk the half-dark, the early mists that obscured the earth and attempt to set the plane down in Central Park. He swept in a wide circle and, flinchingly, gazed down at his fortress home on the East River. Its iron gates stood wide. That was proof enough that it was no longer guarded!—that Nita and the rest had fallen prey to the Master's raiders.

Wentworth's eyes were hard and bitter as he turned back to the task of making a safe landing. He chose the sports field in the center of the park and slanted steeply in. It would have to be swiftly done. Police cars were on constant patrol of the park, and they would speed to investigate. They might be Kirkpatrick's men and loyal to him; or they might be taking orders from Kirkpatrick's successor. He had no way of telling.

The white, rising mists of dawn shredded out before the plane. The motor's rhythm was subdued so that the whine of wind on the struts came through to his ears. He cast a final glance toward the roadways, but failed to spot any police cars; then all his attention was concentrated on landing. The plane took the ground gently under his masterly handling, stopping within a few feet of the trees that girdled the field. Wentworth cut the ignition, sprang to the ground and darted to their cover. His deadened ears picked up the hammer of an automobile engine from the west driveway of the park and he turned to the east and drove his weary body into a lope.

The high windows of buildings were red with the first rays of the sun when, slowing to a walk, he strode out into Fifth Avenue. He found a taxi presently and sped southward. He debated a telephone call to Kirkpatrick and discarded the idea. Such a call might precipitate action against the commissioner, if he still were safe. No question but that it would be intercepted. He could ascertain if Kirkpatrick was in his office… He stopped the cab presently and, from a booth in an all-night restaurant, phoned headquarters. The instant he heard his friend's crisp voice over the instrument, Wentworth hung up. It took will-power to do that. So easy then to blurt out his warning, but it might be fatal to Kirkpatrick. Wentworth raced back to the taxi and sent it speeding toward Centre Street. The sound of Kirkpatrick's confident voice, harassed though it was, buoyed his hopes. He had failed everywhere else. Perhaps, this time, he could strike a successful blow….

WENTWORTH'S LIPS were set bitterly as he hastened toward headquarters. He had decided to risk an open invasion. He could not know to what extent Kirkpatrick still held the reins, but probably no one would try to block his entrance.

Unobtrusively, he loosened his single remaining automatic in its holster though it was useless against the legitimate police. The Spider did not harm honest officers. That added to his risk. His eyes glinted coldly. He peered alertly ahead as the cab swung into Centre Street. A curse leaped to his lips.

"Don't stop," he ordered. "Go right on by and turn the corner two blocks down."

A squad of police stood guard over the entrance, but they were not the familiar blue-clad men of Kirkpatrick. They were the Black Police! Was he already too late then? Wentworth damned himself for failing to chance the phone warning, but dared not try again. When the cab pulled to a halt, Wentworth leaned forward.

"I'm a secret-service agent," he told the driver. "I've got to get into police headquarters without being seen. I'm going to fire some shots into the air. As soon as I have, speed for the corner, double back and pass behind headquarters. Here's twenty dollars."

The driver winked, "Okay, chief," he said. "You want I should stick around afterward?"

Wentworth shook his head with a slight smile. If he succeeded, there would be no need and if he failed, he would have no chance to flee! "No. Get away as fast as you can, for your own safety," he directed quietly.

He lifted his automatic then and fired it into the air—two shots, a pause and a third; then three more as rapidly as possible. The cab leaped forward like a racehorse from the barrier, and, brief seconds later, Wentworth dropped from it within a half block of police headquarters' rear. His reloaded automatic was back in its holster. He slipped quietly along in the half-light of the street. An emergency truck, loaded with police, slammed out of its garage, and Wentworth ducked into a doorway. As soon as it spun the corner, he darted into the garage.

One policeman was on guard. He swung around... and looked into the muzzle of Wentworth's automatic.

"You're taking me to the second floor of headquarters," Wentworth ordered, "as if I were your prisoner."

The man stared at Wentworth with wide eyes, then said falteringly, "I don't get it, Mr. Wentworth. I'll do it, sure—but why?"

Wentworth laughed. This was better luck than he had hoped for. It was one of the regulars who knew him and his friendship for Kirkpatrick.

"The commissioner is in danger," he said curtly. "Those new state police are on guard at the front door. Maybe all over the building—I don't know. I've got to reach Commissioner Kirkpatrick right away."

The man cursed. "Those damned Black Police," he said. "Sure. Let's go."

Despite the officer's apparent willingness, Wentworth watched him warily as they took the iron stairway that led to sleeping-quarters over the garage. From there, a covered bridge went directly to the second floor of police headquarters. At its entrance, Wentworth faced the policeman and held out his hand.

"From here on, I'd better go alone," he said quietly. "If I fail, I don't want to involve you."

The cop wrinkled his forehead. "What the hell is this?" he said gruffly. "Are them Blackies trying to put anything over on the commissioner?"

Wentworth smiled faintly. If only it were no more than that! "Something like it," he agreed. "Go back to your post and, if you have a car, get it ready for immediate flight. Have the engine running."

"Right." The cop started to salute, then grinned. "Anything for the commissioner." He went rapidly down the stairs and Wentworth faced toward the headquarters building, presently was peering furtively up the broad corridor before Kirkpatrick's office. An entire squad of the Black Police was on guard there! God, had they already made Kirkpatrick a prisoner!

IN HIS office, Stanley Kirkpatrick, commissioner of police, stood at bay behind his desk. It was not that he was physically cornered. Only one man, besides himself, stood in the square box of an office which had a barren, military aspect. But the mutual hostility of the men was apparent in the angry blood that tinged their faces.

"I've already given you my answer, Mayor Culkin." Kirkpatrick bit off his words almost fiercely. "I will not surrender this office to any crooked hireling of yours!"

Culkin was a pompous man, more used to underhand maneuverings than this open battle. He puffed, attempted an amiable smile.

"I really can't understand such defiance, Kirkpatrick," he said slowly. "You have no legal right to the office, you know. I haven't reappointed you. If necessary, I can have you ejected forcibly!"

84

Kirkpatrick shook his head slowly. He was standing very stiffly, his arms folded, chin pulled in. Those who knew him best were a little apprehensive when he assumed that pose. They knew then that he was fighting to hold his temper in check. They knew what happened when his anger burst loose.

"Not without a court order, my dear Mayor," he said flatly. "If you attempt it, there will be... *resistance.*"

Culkin lost patience. "What in the hell can you hope to accomplish by this?" he shouted. "A few days more in office at most! You are destroying discipline! Promoting crookedness among the police!"

Kirkpatrick leaned across his desk, laid a palm down gently on its top. "Let's understand each other, Culkin," he said. "You want to eject me so that you can put a crook in my position. You and the Black Police—Governor Whiting, himself—are taking orders from criminals and I know it. Very well, as long as I can prevent it, you shall not have complete control of my men. Now, if you want to call in your Black Police, go ahead!" He laid a hand on a board of push-buttons on his desk. "I will sound the alarm and bring every man of mine in the building to fight them!"

Culkin laughed. "Go right ahead," he said softly. "Every man of yours is under guard!" He turned toward the door, swaggering, his fat shoulders pulled back as far as they could go.

The window glass broke inward with a tinkle that lay strangely across the hostile silence that had fallen in the room, and Richard Wentworth sprang lightly to the floor, his automatic leveled at Mayor Culkin.

"Stay right there, Culkin," Wentworth ordered softly, "or I'll embroider a pattern on that fat stomach of yours—with bullets!"

Mayor Culkin's jowls quivered. He got his shoulders against the door and stood there, gasping. "Kirkpatrick," he said hoarsely, "arrest that man! He's a public enemy!"

Kirkpatrick's face was stern as he swung toward Wentworth. "Put that gun away, Dick!" he ordered coldly.

"Stay where you are, Kirk," Wentworth answered quietly, "and listen to me!" His gun swung impartially from Kirkpatrick to Mayor Culkin. "Kirk, you heard the mayor call me a public enemy, but you don't know what that means yet. Tell him, Mayor Culkin! *Talk, damn you!*"

Culkin started violently; his words came stammering out. "The governor outlawed him," he said rapidly to Kirkpatrick. "All his property has been confiscated. There's a reward of ten thousand dollars for him, dead or alive."

Kirkpatrick stared at Mayor Culkin in amazement, "What the hell are you talking about?" he demanded.

Wentworth laughed softly. "It's the latest device of our friend, the White Face in the Mirror," he said and saw Culkin's countenance grow pale. "By it, he can assure the destruction of anyone who opposes him. The legislature gave the power to Governor Whiting, and he can use it at his discretion. But you left out one thing, Mayor. If a public enemy is brought in dead, the reward is paid... *and no questions asked!*"

Kirkpatrick's face was dark with anger. "But that's damnable!" he cried. "That's something out of the Middle Ages! It's murder!"

"Yes, murder," Wentworth agreed softly. "Kirk, the governor

has made you a public enemy, too. There's ten thousand dollars on your head!"

"Yes!" Culkin's voice rose shrilly with defiance. "You're a public enemy, Kirkpatrick! That's why you must surrender this office at once!"

Kirkpatrick took a long stride toward Culkin, then checked himself. "That is why he's so anxious to get me out of office," he said harshly. "He doesn't want to proscribe me while I'm the police commissioner. But as soon as I'm out... Culkin, I think you're a public enemy. I think you should have your neck wrung right now!"

Culkin squealed in terror. He turned awkwardly toward the door and beat on it with his fists. The ground-glass panel crashed outward to the floor. "Help! Help!" Culkin cried. "They're killing me!"

Wentworth took a long leap forward, but it was too late. Culkin whipped open the door and ran, waddling, toward the hallway where the Black Police stood guard.

"Kill them!" he was screaming now. "Kill them. They're both public enemies, and there's ten thousand dollars to the man who kills them!"

WENTWORTH TWISTED aside from his race toward the door and threw himself at Kirkpatrick. Together they slammed against the side wall of the office—and not a moment too soon. The volley from the corridor sent a hurricane of screaming lead through the doorway. The inkwell on Kirkpatrick's desk exploded, and a dozen bullets powdered the plaster of the wall. White dust floated into the air as the fusil-lade continued.

Kirkpatrick stared at Wentworth and his face was dead white. He said, with difficulty, "It seems that I owe you my life again, Dick."

Wentworth threw a quick glance toward the window. They were cut off from it by gunfire, trapped against the wall. He swore under his breath. He should have had more foresight! But that was foolish. He had saved Kirkpatrick in the only way he could. Any delay for strategy would have meant the commissioner's death.

"We've got to leave here at once," he said curtly. "The building is overrun with Black Police. If we can reach the window, there's a narrow ledge we can walk to the end office, then into the emergency-wagon garage. There's one of your men there and he'll have his car ready, with the motor running."

Kirkpatrick pulled out his long-barreled revolver, "I'm not leaving!" he said grimly.

Wentworth's own automatic was in his fist, and together they kept alert watch on that doorway. Two guns were still firing, fanning the opening with bullets. That meant the rest was creeping nearer for a rush.

"It's no use, Kirk," Wentworth said rapidly. "You can't hold onto the commissionership any longer. I tell you the Black Police have taken over! You're not a citizen of this state any longer. You're an outlaw, with no rights, except the right to die! There won't even be an investigation if you're killed! Ten thousand dollars reward—and no questions asked! We've got to get away."

Kirkpatrick's face was cut with harsh lines and Wentworth knew well the struggle that went on within him. Kirkpatrick had given years of his life to build the New York police into the strongest and most loyally efficient force in the country. To lose them now, with the certainty that all his good work would be destroyed—that criminality and protection would become the duty of his men instead of a thing they fought—was the bitterest blow that could strike Kirkpatrick. Added to that was the knowledge that he would be a fugitive criminal himself; that from now on his hand must be turned against the men he had taught and loved. Wentworth saw his mouth set grimly and he spoke harshly.

"Kirk, if you take a step toward that door, I'll knock you cold! Getting yourself killed won't help. It's selfish! The people need you now more than they ever had! We'll defeat this combination in time. When that's done, the force will need you to restore its strength. Listen to me, Kirk!"

Kirkpatrick smiled thinly. "It's no use, Dick. I'm finished anyway. I can't live your sort of life. If I could help you do the Spider's work, I would. But—" he shrugged—"I can at least create a diversion while you escape. And maybe I can destroy Culkin!"

"I won't leave you," Wentworth threw at him. "If you die here, I do, too! Come on, we'll be fools together!"

Abruptly, the gunfire from outside the door ceased and there was a pounding rush of feet! The Black Police were charging in for the kill—an entire squad of them against two men. Twenty thousand dollars on their heads—and no questions asked of their murderers!

CHAPTER 8
FIGHT TO A FINISH!

WITH A violent thrust, Wentworth hurled Kirkpatrick toward the wall beside the door. That would be the most protected spot. For himself, Wentworth wanted no protection other than his gun. He could use its swift, unerring bullets like a sword blade against the thrusts of the enemy. There was a fierce anger in him and no fear at all. He threw his mocking laughter in their faces and his automatic was ready in his fist. There were seven cartridges—seven messengers of death!

Two men came through the door together. They dove headlong like tumblers, close to the floor, wrenching their guns about to fire while they still were in the air. Wentworth's automatic seemed to swing almost leisurely. He didn't fire first. Only super-trained gunmen could shoot accurately in the middle of such a charge. Wentworth's automatic crashed out twice, and the two Black Police struck the floor limply, already dead. Wentworth dropped to a knee and scooped up one of the revolvers, and his laughter rang out once more.

Kirkpatrick's revolver crashed and outside the door, a man screamed. Three more were jammed in the opening, fighting to get through. Wentworth helped them. His shot caught the middle man in the forehead, wrenched him backward. The other two pumped out frantic bullets as rapidly as they could, without aiming, screaming in their fear. Wentworth's two guns and Kirkpatrick's hammered out together, and the combined blast rocked the office. The doorway was cleared.

Kirkpatrick twisted a white, distorted face toward Wentworth, then abruptly whipped up his revolver and fired! Wentworth's lips cut short a cry that welled to them. The bullet hissed past so close that his temple felt the hot wind of its passage. For a mad moment, he thought Kirkpatrick had lost his mind, was firing upon him… and then he heard the scream. He twisted his head about.

One of the Black Police, leg hooked over the windowsill behind Wentworth, cradled a sub-machine gun in his arms. Its muzzle began to flicker with powder flame—but too late. Already the man, still screaming, was arching backward. The gun kicked higher, higher in his arms, then man and gun were gone. They popped out of sight, plunged downward. In the sudden aching silence of the room, the sound of the killer's landing made a sodden thud.

Kirkpatrick staggered, a palm grinding to his forehead, and Wentworth leaped to his side. "Are you hit?" he gasped. "God, man that machine gun…."

Kirkpatrick's hand dropped like a stick. "Hit? Not by bullets, no, Dick," he said thickly. His stern eyes had become, in brief moments, unbelievably sunken in his head, and there were dark shadows beneath them. He looked old, broken. "Take me out of here, Dick—" his voice died to a whisper—"before I have to kill… my own men."

Wentworth threw a glance at the window. Men were shouting

in the street. Silence within here, except for Kirkpatrick's deep struggling breath that was close to sobs. Were the Black Police all slain? It must be chanced.

Wentworth caught Kirkpatrick's wrist and charged through the door, his own body before that of his friend. He saw then where the sub-machine gun bullets had struck. The two remaining Black Police had been prepared to charge in. They were driven back, pinned bloodily against the wall of the outer office. But more would come from below unless they were fast. So far, the entire battle could not have lasted more than two minutes.

Wentworth swung left and raced along the corridor, dragging the stumbling Kirkpatrick behind him. They whirled into the covered bridge, and Wentworth's gun swung up. Only at the last moment did he manage to stay the shot that threatened. It was the policeman who had helped him before.

"God, sir," he whispered. "God, sir, you almost...."

"The car!" Wentworth snapped. "Your orders were to stay with it!"

The man wheeled and ran drunkenly before them, half-fell down the iron stairway.

Moments later, Wentworth hurled Kirkpatrick into the rear of the sedan and sprang to the wheel. Before he could prevent it, the policeman had thrown himself in beside him.

"I'm with you, sir," he said. "Anyway, my life wouldn't be worth a cent. They'd know you escaped where I was on guard." He grinned whitely, freckles standing out with an almost painful contrast across his cheekbones. "I stay with the commissioner."

THERE WAS no time to stop and put the man out. Wentworth wrenched the wheel about and bore the accelerator to the floor. The light car jack-rabbited toward the corner and, behind him, the guns of the Black Police began to hammer again. Wentworth's brows were knotted in a tight frown.

Where was he going to hide? For himself, there was always escape in disguise if he could reach certain of his hideouts in the Underworld. But Kirkpatrick was too forthright a man, too unbending in his purposes and concepts, to utilize masquerade. The policeman was an added responsibility. His fortress home obviously had been swept clean by the Black Police. They would have guards there and traps, awaiting his return. It would be suicide to go there. It would be equally impossible, without preparation, to escape from the city. The plane in Central Park would not carry three men even if it could be wrested from the guard that undoubtedly had been placed over it.

No, there was no choice for it. Somewhere in New York, they must find a hiding place. Without thinking, Wentworth was doubling and redoubling on his trail, dodging the pursuit at top speed. It would take the police a few moments to organize. Before that time, he must be far away from the neighborhood of the headquarters. The car was roaring now down the Bowery, the clatter of elevated trains overhead. Store fronts were still dark and only a few tattered remnants of humanity walked the pavements. Ahead was Chatham Square and Chinatown....

"Master!" a man's voice cried out from the darkness. *"Sahib!"*

Wentworth ground down on the brakes. He knew Ram Singh's voice instantly, and where Ram Singh was, there would be Nita also! The car wrenched wildly as he fought it to a stop and, from the shadows of a doorway, a fleet, tall figure sprinted toward him. Wentworth flung wide the door.

"Get in!" he ordered, as Ram Singh darted up. "We're pursued. Where is the *missie sahib?*"

"Pursued?" Ram Singh threw a swift glance up the street. "Here is safety—in the stronghold of Chei Hwang-yo."

Wentworth laughed aloud. Of course! He would have remembered Chei Hwang-yo presently. They had sworn friendship to him, those Chinese who owed Chei Hwang-yo allegiance—and there were many of them. In the old Chinese's home, they would be safe for a while. He sprang to the pavement.

"There is an entrance near here?" he demanded while he gestured to Kirkpatrick and the policeman to leave the car.

Ram Singh rushed out directions while he was climbing in behind the wheel. He knew his task without being told. He must take the car away from this neighborhood. His dark eyes turned hauntingly on his master's face.

"The *missie sahib,*" he said brokenly. "On my head be it, master. She is… gone."

"Gone where?"

Rapidly, Ram Singh outlined the things that had happened in his mansion fortress. "While thy servant was loading the boat, as the *missie sahib* had ordered, I heard her cry out. The elevator was slow, slow. When I reached the spot where the *missie sahib* had been, she was gone! There were police in black uniforms. They did not escape! But the *missie sahib*, I do not know!"

Wentworth's heart was leaden within him. He had recognized Nita's planning, in the instant Ram Singh had mentioned the

Chinese—had hoped to hold her in his arms again, no matter for how brief a while. But now....

"What could be done, you did, my warrior, I know," he said heavily. "Go now, and return swiftly. There is work."

Kirkpatrick's hand was on his arm. "They have taken Nita?" he asked curtly. "Then, by God, I am glad I did what I did! Lead on, Dick."

WENTWORTH HEARD the whooping of sirens, and Ram Singh whipped the car from the curb and sent it rocketing straight ahead down the Bowery. He would do that until he was sighted. No, his bravery could not be questioned, but Nita... Wentworth led the way heavily toward the shadows and into the sour, slattern entrance of a tenement down the cellar stairs. The steps were boarded in with tongue-and-groove planking. There was a great deal such boarding in Chinatown. Its frequent joints made it easier to conceal hidden doorways. He found the knothole Ram Singh had mentioned, thrust his finger through and found a loop of string. A pull and a section of the boarding swung free. He led through it and they were in a low tunnel that paralleled the cellar wall. The way led presently downward, into an iron gallery along a great storm sewer.

Wentworth moved like a man in a trance. He had known Nita was a prisoner or worse, but the sight of Ram Singh—the knowledge that it was Nita's planning that made him safe now with Kirkpatrick and the policeman—lent an added weight of sadness. They were groping their way in utter darkness, but Wentworth scarcely noticed the fact. His hand glided along the brick wall on his left. He felt the beginning of a bend.

"Wait here," he said dully and his voice echoed off through the arch of the sewer. "I must go ahead and prepare for you."

Ten slow paces, he took and then he stood and sent his voice before him in the darkness. "One comes seeking," he said. It was the pass-word he had from Ram Singh.

Instantly, a yellow light bloomed in the blackness and, in its glow, Wentworth could presently see a powerfully built Chinese, standing with folded arms, hands tucked into his sleeves. There would be guns here, Wentworth knew.

"Say to your master, the thrice honorable Chei Hwang-yo," Wentworth lapsed into the Mandarin dialect, the Chinese as spoken in Peking, "that one whom he honored with the unworthy title of friend craves the privilege of speech."

"Wentworth *san,*" the Chinese answered, "my master waits. He bade me say that his unworthy and wretched home is yours."

"I bring two friends."

"Shall a man not bring friends into his own home?"

Wentworth felt his heart swell with gratitude toward the old Chinese. Too few white men would do so much in the name of friendship! Wentworth bowed over his clasped hands, then called Kirkpatrick and the policeman forward.

"A friend of mine makes us welcome," he said quietly.

Wentworth followed the Chinese guard through another series of tunnels and cellarways and they came presently into a broad room where a dozen white men and women were stretched upon rude couches. The scent of antiseptic was strong in the chamber and, when he entered, he saw the black-robed figure of the old priest from Poughkeepsie. A smile touched the man's face.

"Ah, my son," he said gently, "I am glad you come in safety."

From the far shadows of the place, two other figures hurried forward, the girl Angela Manteo, and the young tax collector, Jack Wilson. There was a smile on Wilson's face, despite the pallor of his cheeks.

"Sir," he said, "when you go to fight those Black Police, take me with you! These people are their victims, rescued by Miss van Sloan. And we let those damned police capture her!"

A man lifted himself on his elbow from one of the couches—a gaunt, powerfully built man, weakened now by pain. He lifted his other hand in a clenched fist!

"Lead us against those damned police!" he cried. "Lead us!"

His cry echoed through the room and other figures stirred and lifted themselves; men's voices picked up the words. Wentworth's throat closed on the things he wished to say. Despair had drowned him, the Spider who was accustomed to hopeless battle against great odds. But there was no despair here, though these men were crippled with pain, though they had been stripped of everything that was dear to them. Instead they cried out for a leader in the battle against their oppressors. New strength flooded Wentworth.

"You shall be led," he said, his voice choked. "You shall have the chance to strike back! With men like you, we shall overthrow these criminals who rule the state! I swear it!"

A ragged cheer answered him, and Wentworth passed on, his head lifted again, renewed with courage. He would find Nita and

free her; he would destroy the Black Police and their Master…
Wentworth's lips twisted a little. That was madness and well he
knew it. A dozen men, broken in body, hidden beneath the earth
lest they be slain, and with *them*, he hoped to overthrow the
powerful organization that in a few days had destroyed the state?
Self-mockery tortured him. But who else was there to fight? Not
the police, with Kirkpatrick driven from office, outlawed with
a price on his head. Regardless of the odds, he must succeed.

IT WAS in that moment of despair that Wentworth's plan was
born. The Master was a nebulous figure who appeared only to his
lieutenants as a white, ghostly face in a mirror, but his minions
were everywhere. His organization must be destroyed first of
all, crippled through its main strength, which was stolen wealth.
Once his coffers were emptied, the Black Police, the thousand
subordinates, would rebel. Such criminals could be held loyal
only through money and fear. Wentworth would build a greater
fear, and strip them of money!

Well he recognized how great a task lay ahead, but there were
tens of thousands of honest men in the state. They would bear
the brunt of the crime-madness of the Master. More and more,
they would be oppressed and from among them, Wentworth
could muster a secret army. They would have to be armed and
trained. Very well, the state should supply them with money!
They would strike from a hundred coverts against the oppressors and, in the end, they would triumph. They must! There
were untold obstacles to be overcome, but with courage and
perseverance….

Wentworth realized that he had been ushered into the presence of Chei Hwang-yo. The aged Chinese was smiling at him, his face cut with a thousand wrinkles.

"My son," he said in his perfect, even pedantic English, "you have come to me in your trouble as I came to you in mine. I am proud to serve you. My house and all that I have is yours!"

Wentworth was aware of his overwhelming weariness, as he sank upon the cushions Chei Hwang-yo indicated. The relief of sanctuary, after so many hours of flight and battle, loosened his muscles like a drug. He made his formal response to the Chinese, but, in spite of himself, his head nodded.

Chei Hwang-yo laughed. "You do me too much honor, friend," he said softly. "Now you must rest."

Sleep struck Wentworth like a thunderbolt and it seemed only seconds later that a hand, laid gently on his arm, awakened him. Chei Hwang-yo's face was no longer smiling, but gravely lined.

"My son," he said, "I could wish that I had other words for you than I must voice. At sunset tonight, at Union Square, there is to be a public execution of what the state is pleased to call traitors."

Wentworth shook the sleep from his brain and started up. "What time is it now?" he asked quickly.

Chei Hwang-yo gravely indicated a clock whose hands pointed to four o'clock. "I have just received the word, and there is more, my friend."

Wentworth felt all his body grow taut. Somehow, he knew the answer even before he heard the Chinese speak. He drew himself slowly erect and his eyes tightened with pain.

"Tell me," he said slowly.

Chei Hwang-yo nodded. "It is as you have guessed. The first of those to die will be the woman to whom you have given your heart—Nita van Sloan."

CHAPTER 9
GALLOWS FEAST

BY A violent effort, Wentworth controlled the anger that surged through him. His voice was almost steady as he shot out rapid inquiries. He learned that Ram Singh had at last managed to make his way back to the hideout, bringing word of Nita's doom. The news was being broadcast throughout the city by the newspapers and by Black Police who, mounted in armored cars, stopped at street corners to cry out the news. The Master was preparing to show the people the cost of disobedience to his orders. No doubt of that, or that he hoped, by the threat to Nita, to lure Wentworth into a trap!

Well, he would have that opportunity! Wentworth made the resolution, silently. If he allowed the Master to perform his executions, the reign of terror would be complete. This was the course he must follow, to harass the Master at all times; to give the people hope and the courage to fight.

To Chei Hwang-yo, Wentworth said only, "I understand many of my possessions have been brought here. I shall need some of them."

The Chinese eyed him impassively. "My men shall take your orders, Wentworth *san,*" he said. "The gallows has been erected on the north side of the square and two companies of the Black Police are there already."

Wentworth shook his head slowly. "You already have done too much for me. This is my own battle!"

To reach the room where his possessions were stored, Wentworth had to pass through the chamber where the men Nita had rescued were being doctored. He hesitated there. These men would follow him to rescue the woman who had saved them! Then he shook his head. It could not be. They were too few to attack in force; and now one or two men could accomplish more. He and Ram Singh... the Spider!

Wentworth paused beside the couch were Kirkpatrick slept. It would be best that Kirkpatrick knew the plans he had formed in case anything should happen to him in the battle that lay ahead. But if he aroused him, Kirkpatrick would insist on participating in the venture. Wentworth hurried on, and began to search among the things that Nita had brought. Ram Singh presently joined him.

"What are my master's orders?" he asked, gravely. "It is thy servant's hope that he may be permitted to offer his poor life in recompense for his failure."

Wentworth set his hands on the Sikh's broad shoulders. "Both of us may die," he said quietly, "but there is to be no sacrifice. No blame rests upon you. I have made certain plans. Here are grenades, rifles, automatics and ample ammunition, thanks to the *missie sahib*. This is what we will do...."

WHEN THE sunset lay red as blood across the city, there were twenty thousand people packed into the plaza on the north side of Union Square. Many had come of their own volition, drawn by horror; many thousands of others had been herded there by Black Police on horseback who stopped throngs in the street and drove them toward the square like cattle.

They moved restlessly, and the mutter of their voices was like a gathering storm. Scores of mounted Black Police hemmed them in and, on the southern edge of the plaza where they stood, there was a solid phalanx of horsemen. They stood guard before the colonnaded grandstand. It was on top of this that the gallows had been rigged.

"This woman," he thundered, "rebelled against the constituted authorities of the state!"

Hurriedly erected of great timbers, it was no trap-platform that had been built. Two uprights had been braced into place and, across their top—fifteen feet above the level of the roof—there was a cross-piece, like the lintel of a giant's doorway. Over that, dangling ropes had been tossed. Plainly, the victims were to be hoisted by the hang noose and allowed to strangle slowly, their struggles a lesson for the assembled thousands in the square!

Presently, a slow procession turned from Broadway into the midst of the crowd. Before them, Black Police rode with rearing horses, striking out to open a path. There were three limousines and, behind them, flanked by more of the mounted police, was an open truck in which seven people stood, their hands lashed to the sides. One of them was a woman, and of the six who were men, three of them were heavily bandaged and one had his arm in a sling. A mutter like rising wind swept through the crowd. These were the gallows' prey—those who were about to die.

It was strange that, of all those who rode in this new and cruel tumbrel, only the woman kept her head erect. Her lips even managed to move in a smile as she looked down upon the people who gazed upon her. Nita's chestnut curls were loose to the wind and they stirred about her face. If the sight of that brutal gallows shook her, she showed no sign. Instead, she looked beyond them, up at the fiery brilliance of the sky—the jut of buildings that shouldered against it. She had no hope of rescue, did not even know that Richard Wentworth had returned to New York.

She had no regret for the things she had done, nor for the life she had chosen to share with Dick. But it would be hard to die without seeing him once more, without knowing whether he had escaped the traps set for him in Albany. She turned to the man bound beside her.

"It will soon be over now, Jackson," she said quietly.

Jackson turned his soldier's impassive face toward her. He wore his arm in a sling. "If *he's* alive, Miss Nita," he said harshly, "they won't get away with it. Don't you give up hoping, Miss Nita, even when—when they get busy."

Nita smiled then. "It's brave of you, to encourage me," she said simply. "Thank you, Jackson. But even if he's safe—even if he knew about this—what could he do?" Her nod indicated the jammed thousands before the gallows, the close lines of mounted police, a machine gun mounted in the speaker's stand. "Better to hope that he doesn't know!"

They fell silent then as the truck maneuvered and backed up against a flight of steps that led to the roof and the gallows. There was a continuous shouting from the people now. A troop of the police drew their revolvers and fired shots into the air. Nita turned her eyes toward the gallows and the roof. One man there in civilian clothing, the others were high officials of the Black Police, a half dozen in all. Over on the far side of the crowd, a single horseman was pushing his way forward. For a moment Nita's heart leaped with hope and fear. There was something familiar about the erect, masterful way the man sat his horse… but he wore the uniform of the Black Police, an officer of some sort from the glitter of gold at shoulder and sleeve.

ROUGH HANDS seized Nita. Her bonds were slashed loose and she was thrust up the steps toward the gallows, alone.

105

Below, the other prisoners stared upward after her with gaunt and terrified faces. Something close to panic seized Nita, as she was brought to a halt beneath those dangling ropes. Her hands were wrenched around behind, tied again; the rough hemp of the rope rasped her white throat.

Nita bit her lip and lifted her face to pray, but above her was the brutal black line of the gallows against the red of the sky. She choked down a sob. If only she could have seen Dick once more. She thought again of that lone horseman off there in the crowd, but she could no longer see him. The civilian, flanked by the police, had stepped to the edge of the gallows platform, and was lifting his voice. It boomed out over the assembled crowd and a thick, waiting silence fell.

"This woman," he thundered, "rebelled against the constituted authorities of the state—the men you elected to serve you. She was responsible for the deaths of five policemen! She has been duly tried by the state courts and condemned to be hanged, publicly, as a lesson and an example to others who may contemplate lawlessness. This woman is a traitor to the state. She—"

There was the thud of a blow, and the speaker catapulted queerly backward to the roof. He struck so violently that his feet lifted and then clumped down again. They drummed on the metal and the sound that they made was terribly loud in the abrupt quiet. Nita stared at him with her eyes strained wide in a white, frightened face. Between the man's eyes was a bullet hole!

Even as Nita recognized the import of the thing that had happened, the black-clad police officers were falling. Three of them were down, and there still had been no sound of a shot.

The fourth struggled to pull his revolver. A shout that might have been the beginning of an order rose in his throat, but got no farther. A bullet drove him back against the side post of the gallows and he clung there, his face working terribly, through a long moment before he fell. The one remaining officer ran to the edge of the roof and leaped out into space, but, even as he jumped, death was upon him. His body jerked, arms and legs went limp, and he struck the earth as insentient as a shovel full of dirt.

From the ladder by which she had mounted to the gallows, a man's voice spoke with harsh authority. "Bring the prisoner here. At once. It's an attempt to rescue her. Hurry, you fools, before you're killed, too!"

The rope was snatched from Nita's neck and the two executioners thrust her across the roof. A crescendo of pistol shots burst out, but none of them flew near. Nita was staring at the Black Police officer upon the ladder, the man who wore the silver eagle of a colonel upon his shoulder. A cry rose in her throat, but she choked it down.

"Hurry!" the man rasped.

Nita was thrust down the ladder into his arms and the two executioners leaped for safety. Nita's hands were bound behind her, but she gazed up into the face of the colonel of police with eyes that were at once incredulous and laughing.

"Dick!" she whispered. "Oh, Dick… I knew you'd come!"

Wentworth thrust her into the back of the truck, without a word, then mounted to his horse. "Driver!" he shouted. "Take the prisoners away! Fast! It's an attempt to rescue them!" He flashed a sword from its scabbard, flicked it toward the mounted men. "You men surround the truck! Make an opening through the crowd there! Hurry before the attack begins in full force!"

The crowd already was in flight, and the horsemen easily opened a path for the fleeing truck. Wentworth spurred up beside the driver and, around the truck, horsemen began to pitch from their saddles. Bullets whined out of the air from nowhere at all, without a sound except the hiss of their passage, and one after another, the mounted police pitched to the pavement. Long before they reached the verge of the crowd, they were panic-stricken. They put the spurs to their horses and fled, leaving the truck to trundle on with only Wentworth riding beside the cab.

PRESENTLY, HE stepped to the running-board of the truck, jerked open the door and ordered the driver to move over. He took the wheel himself and, an instant later, his automatic's muzzle cracked against the man's skull. Slowly then, as Wentworth tooled the truck through the last fleeing remnants of the crowd, he began to smile. There was a tap on the window in the back of the cabin and he turned, slid the glass aside and looked into Nita's lovely eyes.

"I've cut all the prisoners looser Colonel," Nita said gaily, "and I have them lying on the bottom of the truck. Any further orders, Colonel?"

Wentworth laughed. "None for the present, Captain," he replied, "but when I stop this truck presently—" He caught her hand to his lips and kissed it and there was a pain in his throat at the remembrance of Nita, so brave and pitiful, with that rope about her sweet neck. There had been a while when he had feared he would not arrive in time. It had been no easy matter to find a high officer of the Black Police in such a position that he could be overpowered and robbed of his uniform. There had been a time, too, when he had been afraid Ram Singh, hidden on a roof with a silenced rifle, would not be able to shoot swiftly enough to prevent Nita's death. But now....

Nita laughed at him, at his kiss upon her hand. She waved her narrow white hand until he kissed it again, "Is that strictly according to military code, Colonel?" she asked.

THE EVENING in the underground warrens, to which Wentworth took Nita and the other prisoners, was strangely gay; perhaps the more so because of the horror they all knew ranged the streets above. Wentworth knew that it was a moment stolen before the months of perilous labor to come. Before the dinner Chei Hwang-yo set before them was fairly over, he was summoning the men he had hidden into conference. There he laid before them the plans he had made.

"It will be impossible for us to hide here indefinitely," he said. "Kirkpatrick is going to take a group of you to the Catskill Mountains where both of us have summer camps. There we will prepare a hideout for the army we must train before we can hope to defeat these criminals. Don't worry about arms or money. The state will supply them to you—the state and the Black Police!"

There were muffled cheers in response to that, but Wentworth silenced them quickly. "I am going to call for volunteers to remain in hiding here with me and fight the Black Police and their masters. It will be perilous. Some of us will be killed. But it is necessary. We must keep up the spirits of the people so that, when we can strike, they will rise to help us. We must prevent the collecting of taxes. That entire criminal crew is held together by the hope of loot. If we keep them from getting it, we will do more than any other thing to wreck their morale!"

He went on. "Before you answer, there is one more thing to tell you. Word has just been brought to me that the Black Police have evolved a new weapon. Those who lift their hands against the police, but are not important enough to be outlawed, are being driven into concentration camps. They are herded through the streets like animals, men and women and children. Those of you who served in the war will know what such camps are like, barbed-wire fences and leaky, cold ramshackle buildings, too little food—a dozen people jammed into a space where two could not live healthily. Within a few weeks, there will be disease, a dozen deaths a day.

"These are the people I am asking you to defend at the risk of your own lives. Those who will volunteer...."

A spontaneous shout rang out from all the assembled men. Wentworth laughed, but there were tears in his eyes. With men like these, he could destroy a hundred such criminal governments! He lifted his hands.

"We will divide up the forces this way," he decreed. "Those who are disabled will go with Kirkpatrick, to prepare for the day when we can smash the concentration camps and send the people to hide in the mountains. The rest will stay and fight!"

The crash of the door being thrown open was like a gun-blast. A Chinese ran in and prostrated himself before Chei Hwang-yo where he sat beside Wentworth, and the words poured from his lips in broken sobs.

Wentworth caught his phrases and faced the men before him. "You will have a chance to fight for liberty sooner than I had thought," he said crisply. "Jackson, Ram Singh, open that door and distribute guns and ammunition, while Kirkpatrick and Chei Hwang-yo plan for our defense. The Black Police have tracked us here, and are already breaking down the doors!"

CHAPTER 10
BATTLE IN THE DARK

NOTHING OF the despair that swept him showed in Wentworth's firmly lined face. The men cheered as they rushed for the arms that Ram Singh and Jackson were distributing. "Shame be upon my head," Wentworth said to Chei Hwang-yo. "I have brought destruction upon you!"

The Chinese smiled slightly. "The way to the river is still open," he said quietly. "Do you and your friends fly that way while my men hold back the enemy. They are at the doors, but it will be long before they reach here. I have taken certain necessary precautions long ago."

"The way to the river," Wentworth echoed softly. Suddenly, he laughed aloud. "Chei *san*, honorable father," he said, "this place would not long have been safe for you with the human rats who burrow toward us now. It will be safe again as soon as we have wiped them out. We must retreat... by way of the river! We move sooner, instead of later, to the fastnesses of the mountains! Let them follow us there if they dare!"

Kirkpatrick and the aged Chinese stared at him. Nita's hand closed on his arm and clung there, while Wentworth raced on.

"We can operate from a base there, strike equally well at Albany or New York," he cried. "Within a few days, we can be fortified so strongly that they cannot drive us out! Nita, set the men to carrying arms and ammunition to the river passage. Fasten them in bundles that men can sling over their shoulders! Ram Singh, take five men and fight as rearguard against these Black Police until we are clear."

"My son forgets," said the Chinese slowly. "We cannot run through the city streets with arms on our backs. Even if we could find enough cars, they would be stopped by the armored trucks and machine guns of the police."

Wentworth laughed aloud, in triumph. "That is the easiest part of all," he cried. "Near the place where your river door opens, there is a fireboat, which keeps steam up all the time. There is only a small crew on board, the rest on shore in the firehouse. If we strike fast, we can seize it before an alarm is given... And fire boats are speedy—they have to be!"

Kirkpatrick's lips parted in a wide smile. "Give me three men, Dick, and we'll bring that fireboat to the river door."

Chei Hwang-yo lifted a hand that trembled a little and removed his glasses, symbol of his age and wisdom. He bowed.

"You are my elder brother," he told Wentworth, then he turned and his voice crackled with orders. Within moments, Chinese were scuttling everywhere, salvaging treasure and arms, trotting off along the way toward the river. Somewhere a man screamed, hoarsely, terribly. Chei Hwang-yo smiled a little. "My arrangements... still fight for us," he said gently. "We have plenty of time."

Within ten minutes, everything that could be moved had been fastened into bundles for men's backs and was being sped toward the river door. Ram Singh's party was shooting now, the crash of their guns echoing through the dark caverns below the city streets. Nita ran to Wentworth's side.

"The boat has left the dock!" she cried. "The men are waiting to leap aboard. Call Ram Singh in."

"It is time," Chei Hwang-yo agreed. "Even when we have left, my *arrangements* will fight for us. You need not fear pursuit from these men, my elder brother!"

Wentworth had fought his way through the warrens of hostile Chinese before this, and he had some knowledge of the horrors that lay in wait for the Black Police. It was not his way of fighting, but he could feel no sympathy for those criminal cohorts, most of them recruited from the penitentiaries whose doors the crooked governor had thrown wide. Together, the aged Chinese, Nita and Wentworth made their way along the storm sewer that led to what Chei Hwang-yo called his "river door." Ram Singh and his men closed in behind them, a great metal barrier slid down behind them in rubber-sealed grooves. It dimmed the sounds behind, but even so Wentworth could hear thin, rising screams. They did not continue for long....

Nita's face was pale when, at the mouth of the sewer, he

handed her up a ladder thrown overside from the fireboat. Kirkpatrick called down cautiously from the wheelhouse.

"We'll have to hurry," he said. "They might send my own men after us."

Wentworth's voice cracked out, hurrying the last of the men aboard. No, they could not fight the regular police. They were honest men, and fearless, a different breed from these renegade Blacks. Moments later, the fireboat swung out into the stream. The tide was setting in and they sped northward with the double drive of current and engines. Fortunately, the night was black. Let them once distance pursuit and gain the wide reaches of the Sound and, until daylight, they would be safe enough.

WENTWORTH HURRIED up to the wheelhouse and found there one of the men he had saved from the gallows—a red-faced, broad-shouldered fellow who seemed utterly at home where he was. He grinned, touched his forelock.

"You don't need to worry as long as Sailor Joe is at the wheel, Mr. Wentworth," he said, with a wink. "I know these waters like the palms of my hands."

"Good!" Wentworth nodded. "Take her into the Sound, Joe. Keep well out from both shores and give all boats a wide berth." He remained for a moment beside the wheel and watched the competent movements of the man's blunt-fingered weathered hands. He glanced out the windows, then uttered a startled exclamation.

"One of your police boats, Kirk!" he cried. "It's overtaking us fast!"

Kirkpatrick swore under his breath. "We can't fire on them!"

he said resolutely. "They're honest men, Dick, not scoundrels like those black uniformed killers."

"You're right," Wentworth agreed swiftly, "but I have a plan. You talk with them when they come within hail, Kirk. They won't open fire on you." As Kirkpatrick hurried out, Wentworth turned to the helmsman. "Joe, listen for my hail. When you hear it, stop the engines. When I shout again, full speed ahead. And stop for nothing!"

The man winked his cheerful blue eyes again. "Aye, aye, sir," he agreed. "Stop the engines at the first hail; full speed ahead at the second, and stop for nothing!"

Wentworth raced out of the wheelhouse and shouted for Jackson and Ram Singh. The police boat was drawing rapidly nearer now and Kirkpatrick stood at the rail, faring it. A pistol shot rang out.

"Aboard the fireboat!" The hail came from the police launch. "Heave to!"

Wentworth sent a low-voiced hail to the wheelhouse, felt the pulse of the engine die, then raced toward the bow. Ram Singh was clambering to the roof of the wheelhouse, Jackson slipping to the stern. Far down in the hull, machinery began to throb as Wentworth signaled the engine room. The firemen operators were still aboard, under guard of his men. Assured of safety, and early release by Wentworth, they had agreed to work the boat and they had responded promptly.

Kirkpatrick answered the police hail, "I'm Commissioner Kirkpatrick," he called crisply. "I've commandeered this boat. Sheer off and convoy us."

The hail that came back was respectful. "Sorry, Mr. Kirkpatrick, our orders are to arrest you and everyone with you. Unless you surrender, we'll be compelled to open fire!"

Forward, Wentworth was swiveling the hose-nozzle of the bow water-gun toward the approaching boat which was running close under the rail now. Atop the pilothouse and in the stern, Ram Singh and Jackson were doing the same. These guns could hurl a three-inch column of water a hundred and fifty feet into the air, and the police launch was less than fifty feet away, drawing closer. Kirkpatrick was haranguing the men.

Cautiously, Wentworth reached out and tapped a single light peal from the watch-bell forward. At the same instant, he wrenched open the valve of the water-gun; Jackson and Ram Singh did the same. The converging columns of water struck the launch with fierce force. Wentworth's stream smashed the glass from the pilothouse, drove the helmsman in a backward somersault into the cockpit. Ram Singh's water-gun, depressed from the roof, beat the sergeant to the floor and the combined wash hammered the police relentlessly about in the bottom of the cockpit.

For nearly a minute, while the men scrambled to get to their feet and loose their gunfire on him, Wentworth continued to deluge the launch. Only when he heard the launch's motor splutter and die as it was drowned out by the flood did he shout to Sailor Joe in the wheel-house. The fireboat had not lost way entirely and quickly picked up speed, while the water-guns continued to play over the launch until it dropped out of range. It was the only challenge to their escape. Apparently, no

116

other boat was near enough to reach them before they charged through Hell Gate and out into the black reach of the Sound.

As soon as he was sure they were out of immediate danger, Wentworth called a conference in the cabin, outlined his plans. "BEGINNING AT midnight," he told the assembled men, "we'll land small parties at various points near Connecticut towns. You'll carry your quota of arms and supplies and be given expense money. Each of you will be under charge of two leaders, one of whom will remain in hiding with the men. The other will make his way into the nearest town and as soon as possible, buy a second-hand truck. You will then proceed to certain rendezvous in the Berkshire Hills. The routes will be marked out for you.

"I will arrange for each group to be met then and guided to the hideout. Once we are established there, not even the Black Police will be able to destroy us. And we need not worry about food or supplies—for the Black Police will finance us, too! Get what sleep you can now."

The men gave Wentworth a brief, muffled cheer and filed out. Their morale was good, Wentworth was glad to see. The facility of the rescue from the gallows, the escape from the underground trap and the defeat of the police launch had given them faith in his leadership....

Wentworth, with Kirkpatrick and Nita, worked swiftly through the night, deciding on leadership and routes. Dawn was scarcely arrived when it was time to begin disembarking the groups.

There were two rowboats and with these the landings on deserted shores were accomplished. It was necessary to move warily to avoid possible police patrols. The radio brought news of rioting throughout New York and of planes questing for the stolen police boat.

Wentworth had no fear of being spotted by the planes during the blackness of the overcast night, but he knew that with the dawn, their safety would be at an end. Nevertheless, the east was rosy-colored with the rising of the sun when the last group of men was put ashore near Bridgeport—and for him the most desperate part of the venture now began. He had waited until last, and Nita insisted on remaining. The last man ashore, and Nita at the wheel, Wentworth took command of the engine-room, gun in hand. He sent the fire-boat speeding southeastward toward the Long Island shore.

It was necessary to delay, as long as possible, any pursuit in Connecticut, for it would be impossible for the men to make purchases of trucks and cars until nine o'clock or later. License plates must afterward be bought, and then the long trek into the hills begun. Kirkpatrick would take charge there until Wentworth's arrival. But meantime… Wentworth started at the shrill whistling of the speaking-tube and bent toward it to hear Nita's terse voice.

"Two planes coming this way," she reported. "I think they're New York police ships."

Wentworth glanced at his watch. It was eight o'clock, and they were in mid-Sound. The police had one amphibian plane and might attempt a landing; probably they would content themselves with radioing New York for police launches. Abruptly, a smile stirred Wentworth's lips. He eyed the three men in the engine-room, then set swiftly to work. He ordered one man to bind the other two.

"You'll be free in a few moments," he reassured them. "The police planes are coming now."

He stopped the boat's engines, called up the speaking-tube to Nita to keep out of sight until he was ready. Then he faced the third fireman and, emptying the cartridges from a revolver, handed the weapon to him.

"You're going to take me, a prisoner, up on the deck," he said, "and signal to those planes. Put on your uniform cap."

The man grinned wryly. "You're going to fix it so I'll be kicked out of the department," he said. "Pension gone and all the rest of it. That's a hell of a note, Mr. Wentworth."

Wentworth nodded somberly. "I'm sincerely sorry," he said. "I could offer you money, but that would be bribery. I can only tell you this. Sooner or later, the crooked regime that has control of the state will be thrown out of office. When it does, I'll see that you get your job back. If I'm not... still around, then Commissioner Kirkpatrick will attend to it. That goes for all of you men. If you're honest, you know that criminals have seized control of the government. Because Kirkpatrick opposed them, they've made him an outlaw with a ten-thousand-dollar price on his head." He nodded to the man who had protested. "Your name? Frank Connors? All right, Connors. On deck."

Wentworth led the way to the deck, the empty gun pointed at his back, careful not to allow Connors to come close enough to strike. He lined up against the railing then, hands lifted.

"When the plane comes near enough," he directed, "hail

them. They probably won't be able to hear you, but point to the engine-room, then to me. Hold up your fingers, spread out, and try to indicate to them that you have fifteen prisoners there and need help."

Connors' face was pale. "I'll try, sir, but if those are Black Police, they're going to kill me when you're gone. You want them to land so that you can take the plane?"

Wentworth nodded, eyes keenly on Connors' face. It was an honest face, though deeply lined now with worry.

"Look, Mr. Wentworth," he hurried on, "let me go with you! I hate these crooks as much as you do! I'll be glad to fight them! I know you have no reason to trust me, but if Mr. Kirkpatrick is in with you, then, damn it, I am, too!"

Wentworth smiled slowly, "I'd shake your hand for that, Connors, if they couldn't see us. It's a deal! But remember, it's a long fight that lies ahead of us. There will be death for some of us."

"I'm not afraid of death, sir, if it's honorable!"

Wentworth nodded again and his heart was more buoyant for the faith that the man expressed. Criminals couldn't continue to rule, when honest men felt that way. They needed only a leader and, heaven helping, he would lead them! The two police planes were swooping near now and Connors began to wave his hands frantically at them, shouting and gesturing as Wentworth had ordered. The land plane swung in a wide circle, then sped back toward New York. The amphibian swooped nearer, motor cut and struts whining with the wind, as it swept past the fire boat.

"Prisoners!" Connors shouted. "Ten prisoners. I'm alone!"

THE PLANE picked up and circled again while Connors continued to gesture despairingly. Abruptly, Wentworth leaped toward Connors and wrested the gun from him, pretending to strike him over the head.

"Lie quietly," he said sharply. He darted toward the wheelhouse, with a backward-flung glance toward the plane. This time, he had accomplished his purpose. The amphibian was slanting swiftly to a landing. He heard the popping of police guns faintly, and lead whined past his head—but he made the pilothouse.

"As soon as the plane lands," he told Nita rapidly, "get to a water-gun and bring it to bear. Don't loose it unless I tell you. We need that plane!"

He darted out then and ran back toward the engine-room, and bullets began to plunk into the bulkhead in his path. He pretended to be frightened, dodged back. The amphibian took the water easily and plowed straight toward the fireboat. For the first time, Wentworth could make out the uniforms of the two men in the cockpit, and his lips thinned. *Black Police!* He flung himself prone on the deck and held his automatic ready. Bullets gouged splinters from the deck, and one sliced across his cheek.

Wentworth sent three shots, carefully wide of the mark, toward the men in the plane. When next they fired, he cried out hoarsely and slumped limply to the deck. The Black Police raised a triumphant shout and continued to pump bullets toward him as the ship slued around and one man climbed out on the wing. He poised then for the final shot that would make certain Wentworth was dead.

Wentworth started to jerk up his gun, but, before he could

fire, the Black killer's bullet drove down through his right shoulder. Numbness raced through his side, his hand relaxed about his gun. Desperately, he shifted it to his left hand. The policeman was laughing, taking his time with a final, murderous shot....

The crack of the gun came from far forward, where Nita had taken her stand—and her aim was true. The Black Policeman pitched backward off the wing. His hands clawed frantically for a moment at the fuselage and then he hit the water with a violent splash. He went straight down. Wentworth pushed himself to his knees, leveled his automatic at the pilot of the plane.

"Surrender!" he cried.

The man's answer was a hoarsely shouted challenge and the crash of his gun, as he grabbed for the throttle. He never reached it. Wentworth's gun jerked in his hand. He slipped and almost fell, but the bullet sped true. The pilot reared out of his seat and slumped over the edge of the cockpit, instantly dead. For a moment, Wentworth stared toward the man. Then, fumblingly, he pushed himself to his feet, lips shut grimly against the tearing agony that was beginning to run through his shoulder and down his back. Wentworth gestured with the automatic, "Make the plane fast to us," he ordered Connors, and watched while the man did the job. He showed no inclination to hold back, or to attack him. Nita's feet beat swiftly along the deck.

Then she stopped.

"Dick!" she cried. "Dick, you're wounded! Is it—"

"Cracked my shoulder blade, I think," Wentworth told her slowly. "Tie me up the best way you can, and we'll get away from here. You can pilot the plane. You know where to go...."

Minutes dragged past, while Nita worked over his shoulder. "The bullet went straight through," she said, with relief. "But your shoulder blade does seem to be fractured."

Connors stood white-faced before Wentworth, his lips taut, "What do you want me to do, sir?" he asked quietly. "You made it possible for me to stay aboard by attacking me like that. Is that what you want?"

Wentworth nodded, fighting for clarity of thought against the pain that was racking him. "It would be better. Smash the radio. Head the boat for New York. Delay your report as long as possible, without drawing suspicion to yourself. They should give you a medal. Tell them you wounded me."

Connors said slowly, "I'd prefer to go with you, but if I can serve you better this way, then I will. At least, I can gather information in New York City for you."

Wentworth held out his left hand and gripped that of Connors'. "You won't lose by this, I promise you," he said.

It was laborious for him to climb along the wing and into the cockpit, but Nita's bandages had stopped the bleeding. As soon as he was seated, she climbed in and eased the throttle of the still idling plane, sent it skimming over the water. Wentworth glanced at his watch. It lacked only a few minutes of nine o'clock, and satisfaction lighted his eyes. Within the next half hour, the last of his men should have started for the hills. It would be a great deal longer than that before the police got the truth from Connors.

He turned his head toward Nita, and smiled. There was a

smile on her lips, too. The wind tossed curls about her face, and her mouth shaped soundless words, "We'll win now!"

CHAPTER 11
THE GROWING TERROR

NITA GUIDED the plane with consummate skill to a landing on the lake near Wentworth's Catskill camp. Kirkpatrick arrived soon afterward and helped her get Wentworth into bed. It was twenty-four hours before the last contingent of men reached the hideout, though only one party ran into difficulties. They had been forced to shoot their way clear, but none of the police had been killed. Even after that arduous flight, there could be no rest.

Wentworth found himself with a band of forty men and women hidden out in the mountain fastnesses. There were crowded sleeping accommodations for all in the large hunting lodge, but food was an immediate problem as was the ever-present danger that they would be spotted by the Black Police. Of these forty, twelve were Chinese who had come with Chei Hwang-yo, nine of them servants, three others good fighting men. Of the white men, the nine Nita had saved from the floggings of the Black Police, and the six Wentworth had snatched from the gallows, were all partly crippled by the mistreatment they had undergone. But none hung back on that account from the work.

Though Wentworth was forced by Kirkpatrick to remain in bed, he swiftly organized the camp. Jack Wilson and the policeman, Cassidy, who had elected to flee with Kirkpatrick, were dispatched with one of the trucks to buy foodstuffs at some remote point; Ram Singh and the three Chinese warriors were posted as sentries. The women, of whom there were three besides Nita and Angela Manteo, took over the operation of the house. The remaining men set to work to build shelters for the trucks, hidden in the woods from airplane observation; to cut firewood and enlarge quarters; to erect barricades for defense in case of attack. Even the diminutive priest, Father Flower, kirtled up his robes and swung an ax with the rest, and the men sang as they worked.

When these things had been arranged, Wentworth could think for a moment of the future. They were reasonably safe here from a concerted attack by the Black Police—so long as they were content to remain here and keep hands off the oppressors. But that was far from the Spider's intention. He had the nucleus of a strong fighting force and a fair armament for them. Nita had carried off a small arsenal from his home; Chei Hwang-yo had contributed other guns. There were a dozen rifles already in the hunting lodge and, in addition, two submachine guns. With discipline established, and the men trained in marksmanship, they should be able to defend themselves adequately.

But all that would take time. Meanwhile the oppressors were gaining in strength, the criminal Master was cementing his power in the cities and people were being tortured, stripped of their meager wealth. With the urgency of his thoughts, Wentworth stirred restlessly in the bunk to which the weakness of his wound confined him. As soon as he could regain his strength,

125

he must leave this organization and fortification to others, to Kirkpatrick. For himself, he must push on with the ceaseless warfare to which he had eternally dedicated himself. He must find and destroy the Master. He must snatch their victims from the Black Police.

Already he was convinced that no single, sharp blow could smash the swiftly waxing power of the criminals. Here, in these fastnesses, they would assemble an army that would end by destroying Whiting and Culkin and their murderous Black Police!

Nita's voice called to him cheerfully, and he rolled his head to see her entering with a great arm-load of spruce with which she began to decorate the barren, rough hewn logs of the walls. The fresh cold of the high altitudes, against which a fire blazed on the field-stone hearth, had brought warm color to Nita's cheeks.

"I think the people are completely happy," she called to him. "It's like something out of the past—Robin Hood in the green forest of Sherwood." She crossed to him. "Only, Robin is wounded and out of the battle."

A smile softened Wentworth's lips, but grimness lay darkly in his eyes. "The feudal lords of those days never mistreated the serfs any more cruelly than the Black Police do in these days," he said somberly. "I'm afraid our task is more difficult, too. Robin Hood at least knew whom he had to defeat. It won't accomplish much to battle against the Black Police, unless we can learn the identity of the Master and crush him. And this confounded shoulder of mine...."

Nita bent toward him. "The work doesn't need to stop, Dick," she said urgently. "You can accomplish a thousand times more by remaining here in the hills until you get your strength. You can plan for the men, send out spies. I'll go myself."

Wentworth moved impatiently. It must be so, until he could recover from this wound.

BUT THE days that followed were torture for him. News began to trickle in, from the men they sent out and over the circumscribed press broadcasts of the radio. Three big concentration camps had been established by the Black Police and already were jammed to overflowing. The suffering of the people aroused Wentworth to fury. But he could do nothing, nothing, until his magnificent body had mended itself.

The fireman, Frank Connors, was sending a constant stream of information through the contact Wentworth had established.

Under the stringent new tax laws, the people were being drained of their resources, tortured and beaten when they resisted. And Mayor Culkin had devised a new means of extorting money. Wentworth heard his oily voice over the radio as he proclaimed the "Save-a-Life Relief Fund," with a goal of ten million dollars!

"This state takes care of its own unemployed and poverty-stricken," Mayor Culkin intoned. "Its citizens are generous—very. In raising this great fund, there will be no solicitation of the people, no canvassers. We are sure that will not be necessary. Instead, we invite those who wish to make gifts to come to City Hall Square and turn in their contributions in person. To each person will be given the Order of the Purple Cross, a medal which we are going to ask all donors to wear prominently.

On the back of each medal will be stamped the amount of each man's gift...."

Wentworth swore harshly as the mayor's smooth voice rolled on. "That's the most diabolical thing I ever heard," he said sharply. "You see what he intends? His Black Police will patrol the town, and every person who doesn't wear that Purple Cross will be persecuted! Furthermore, they'll be afraid to make small contributions because the amount is to be stamped on the medal! And all very neat and within the law. Mayor Culkin, the Black Police, and the Master, will have ten million dollars to play with!"

Kirkpatrick's own lips were grimly set "It's time we took some action, Dick," he said. "Though, I'll admit, I don't see what we can hope to accomplish against Mayor Culkin and his Purple Cross campaign!"

Wentworth stood and deliberately loosened the sling from his right arm. His face went white with pain as he lowered it to his side.

"Not you, Dick!" Kirkpatrick said sharply. "You're not strong enough for it yet."

Wentworth's pallor came from more than pain. His voice was strained, subdued. "I'm afraid you're right," he said, "but no more can you make an attack in force on Culkin and the Black Police. We aren't ready yet. I have the beginning of a plan. We'll need money, arms, more men... and by heavens, the Black Police shall supply us with what we need—the arms and money. For the men, there are the concentration camps!"

The men grouped about the fire in the big main room of the

camp had fallen silent, but at Wentworth's words they broke into a cheer. Wentworth smiled at them, turned to Kirkpatrick.

"We've been idle too long," he said, in an undertone. "We've information here we can work on. The monthly payroll of the Black Police will be assembled in Albany tomorrow. We'll steal that—and use it to defeat them! There has been a police arsenal assembled in New York City. We'll loot that! Then smash open the concentration camp nearest the city, arm the men…."

"And seize control of the city government!" Kirkpatrick cried.

Wentworth shook his head. "Useless, unless we can identify the Master and eliminate him," he said. "Governor Whiting would send the national guard against us. We couldn't fight them. They're not criminals like the Black Police. They're honest men like your own cops, doing their duty."

Kirkpatrick frowned heavily. "Then what can we accomplish, aside from harassing them?"

Wentworth smiled, leaned closer, "The loss of their loot will do more to disrupt the Black Police than any amount of sniping we can do!" he said. "What we'll do is to seize that ten million and give it back to the people from whom it was stolen!"

THANKS TO the men he had sent out as spies, Wentworth had a very complete picture of the handling of the Black Police monthly payroll. It was distributed from Albany. Each substation of the police sent two men to the capital and it was their job to return the money to the stations. For the work, Wentworth chose the men who had been snatched from the gallows and some of those who had been flogged. He addressed them privately.

"I am choosing men who know the true nature of those we fight," he told the ten he had chosen, "for this reason. When we reach Albany, we will scatter. It will be each man's job to get a Black Police uniform. Any of you who has scruples against… attacking one of the Black Police may be excused now."

Wentworth's keen eyes swept the faces of the men assembled before him and the grimness of them gave him his answer, even without the low, angry murmur of assent.

"Very well," he agreed. "We are going in one truck. If police stop us that will reduce the labor of our search for uniforms by so much."

Sailor Joe was one of those Wentworth had chosen, and he threw back his head in a deep-throated laugh. "I like the talk of you, sir. I'll vow I do!"

Wentworth laughed with him. "You are brave men," he said finally. "You have suffered. Tonight, you will have a chance to avenge yourselves somewhat. But remember this, I must have obedience, complete and absolute. I do not threaten you, but I warn you this: The slightest delay in following a command may doom us all!"

In spite of the necessity of carrying his arm in a sling, Wentworth was determined to lead this first foray against the enemy himself, both for the sake of the morale of the men and to be sure that nothing went wrong. If they failed in this first attempt, it would seriously damage the spirit of the whole group. He had trained the men as carefully as possible. They had been drilled like soldiers by Jackson and Kirkpatrick and trained to shoot with deadly accuracy.

Wentworth rode in the cab beside the driver as the truck trundled off toward Albany, and it was already twilight when they began to roll into the city's outskirts. Wentworth stopped the truck then, spoke briefly to the men.

"As soon as you get uniforms, put them on," he ordered. "I'll expect you all to meet me in one hour at the place you know. If any is delayed longer than that, he will have to make his way back to the camp as best he can. We cannot wait."

There was a low murmur of assent from the men and they scattered into the early dusk except for Sailor Joe who would remain with Wentworth. At Wentworth's signal, the driver of the truck turned about and headed back for the hills. Watching it go, Wentworth knew a curious sense of desertion. That was the last link that bound them to the safety of their mountain encampment. From this point, they were on their own.

Sailor Joe growled, "Orders, sir?"

"Find some of the Black Police!"

Side by side, they walked rapidly toward the center of the city. Once, an armored truck patrol passed at high speed, and they had a glimpse of black uniforms within. Sailor Joe swore under his breath, but Wentworth shook his head. This was not at all what they were looking for.

It was a half dozen blocks farther on that they heard a woman scream, and Wentworth's left hand closed on Sailor Joe's arm.

"I think we've found our quota of Black Police!" he said softly.

They rounded a corner toward the sound, and Wentworth spotted the armored truck parked before an elaborate residence. The woman cried out again in hysterical pleading. The door of the house stood open and light laid in a yellow trapezoid on the stone steps. A black-uniformed guard lounged in the doorway and there was another on the truck.

"Four inside the house," Wentworth said softly. "Joe, you go straight ahead along this side of the street and double up behind the truck. Take the driver without shooting if you can. I'll handle the man in the door...."

"And then, sir?"

Wentworth smiled thinly, "I think we'll pay a surprise visit to the gentlemen inside!"

Sailor Joe's voice was hearty. "Aye, sir!"

THEY SEPARATED, and Wentworth walked steadily toward the house. A man screamed tearingly, and the woman's broken pleading went on and on. Wentworth felt his lips tightening. He had to force himself to a slower pace. He must give Sailor Joe time to reach the truck unobserved. So far, the Black Police guard had paid no attention to his approach. It told, more plainly than any words, how little they had to fear from most of the citizenry.

Wentworth was within twenty feet of the steps to the house before the guard spotted him. "Hey, you!" he called out roughly. "What you doing sneaking up in the dark?"

"I didn't mean to sneak," Wentworth said humbly. "I was just walking by."

"Walking by, huh?" the man snarled. "You come up here and give an account of yourself!"

That suited Wentworth exactly, but the continued cries from within were drawing his nerves taut. He could hear the sickening sound of a whip striking flesh. He went up the steps slowly, cringingly. Up his left sleeve, he carried a blackjack with its loop about his wrist. If he could get close enough… Out of his eye corners, he saw the driver of the armored truck peering toward him. That was fine for Sailor Joe. If they could only time their attack together….

"Hurry up, you!" the guard said raspingly. He knotted his fist threateningly. "How much money you got?"

"None at all," Wentworth said with what sounded like abject fright. "The tax collector was at my house today, and…."

He caught the sound of a deadened blow in the direction of the truck. The guard whipped his head that way and, in the same instant, Wentworth sprang forward. The blackjack slid out of his sleeve and its weight across his palm was good. The guard uttered a startled shout, grabbed for his holstered gun and Wentworth drove the blackjack home to his skull.

Wentworth glanced up, and Sailor Joe's round, ruddy face was grinning at him from the cab of the truck. "Nice work, sir!" he whispered. "This bird won't bother nobody again!"

"Into the truck," Wentworth snapped. "Quickly." He seized the collar of the guard and dragged him forward. Sailor Joe caught up the body and heaved it callously into the back of the truck. "And *he* won't bother nobody neither. Well, there's our two uniforms."

Wentworth was already facing toward the house. "Yes," he said softly. "But some of our men may not be so fortunate. I think there are four men who shouldn't be needing their uniforms much longer!"

Wentworth slid his automatic into his left hand, for he still carried his right in a sling. "Just follow me," he said, and led the way silently into the house. The man's voice broke out in a sudden, broken cry. "In God's name, leave my wife alone! I've given you my last cent! I swear there's not another penny… *Ooh!*" It was a gasp of agony, and it echoed the meaty thud of the whip.

Wentworth was in the main hallway of the house and the sound came from a lighted doorway to the rear. He moved toward it softly; Sailor Joe whispered oaths at his elbow. A moment later, he was peering cautiously into the room, and the thing he saw ripped from him all thought of caution.

A woman, stripped of her clothing, was dangling unconscious from ropes that, bound to her thumbs, had been looped over a door. Her back was laced with crimson whip welts. The man was on his knees before an officer of the Black Police who gripped a stained whip. There was blood on the man's face and on his back. Three other police lounged in evident enjoyment in chairs tipped back against the wall.

"I'll rip the skin off her back, if you don't cough up," the officer said. He drew back the whip again… and it was then Wentworth acted.

He sprang into the room and fired in the same instant. The heavy bullet smashed between the officer's eyes and blew him kicking against the wall. Simultaneously, Sailor Joe opened fire. There was a brief thunderous crashing of guns, and then Sailor Joe was lifting the woman tenderly down from her torture rack.

"I'm afraid, sir," he said hoarsely, "that I ruined one of them uniforms!"

The man looked up with dazed eyes, "In God's name," he whispered. "What have you done? They'll murder us now!"

Wentworth's lips were tight with fury. "Have you a car?" he asked harshly. "Can you drive?"

The man shook his head. "I could drive, yes, but I have no car. Nothing."

"Doctor her up as best you can," Wentworth told him gently. "Get yourself a car and drive to Numbersville. Here's money to buy the car, but make it fast. Take these men's guns with you."

The man stared at the money, took it slowly. "Thank you. Oh, thank you!" he sobbed. "But I don't understand!"

Wentworth forced his lips to relax in a smile. "I'm Richard Wentworth," he said. "There will be safety for you in Numbersville. My men will come for you. Joe, cart out these uniforms. Leave the bodies here."

When the three had gone from the room, Wentworth fingered out a cigarette lighter from his pocket. If these people ever talked, the thing he was about to do would doom him. But the Black Police must feel terror, too—the terror of reprisals! He would frame some story to cover it. He stooped rapidly beside the dead men and, on the forehead of each, he imprinted the burning red seal of the Spider!

Swiftly, then he hurried from the house. Sailor Joe was at the wheel of the truck, clad in one of the uniforms and Wentworth swiftly donned another of them.

HE KNEW it was madness to tempt the fates further in this town overridden by brutal forces who had, at their command, all the strength of the law. But the scene he had just witnessed, drove Wentworth beyond caution.

Further examples of the police brutality were not far to seek. They had not driven a dozen blocks before, once more, cries and the vicious *thwack* of whips caught Wentworth's ear. They turned a corner and, two hundred yards away, caught sight of a piteous procession. A dozen men and women, fastened together in single file with chains about their necks, were being herded along the street by three Black Police on horseback. The first man in the chained procession was being forced to carry a placard on which a small attached light was focused. As Wentworth sent the truck toward them, he made out the legend upon it, painted in fiery red letters. *We didn't pay the tax. We are going to the slackers' camp.*

"The concentration camp," Sailor Joe mumbled. "That's where they're going. Do we take them, sir?"

As Wentworth hesitated, one of the Black Police deliberately spurred his horse against that marching line and rode one of the men to the ground. Two others were dragged down by their chains and, at once, one of the other two police leaped to the ground and began to belabor them with his whip until the victims staggered to their feet.

"Yes," said Wentworth harshly, "We take them! Show them the same mercy they show those poor wretches. As soon as you are alongside of them, stop the truck and shoot. I don't imagine gunshots in this town attract much attention. If they do—well, we are the Black Police!"

A few seconds later, Sailor Joe pulled the truck to a halt. He fired once; Wentworth twice. The chained prisoners stared at them with frightened eyes. Wentworth hurriedly searched the Black Police who wore a sergeant's chevrons and found the keys to their shackles, freed the leading man.

"Unlock the others," he ordered curtly. "Here is money. We'll leave you these men's guns. Get hold of cars and go to Numbersville. You will be protected. If anyone asks who freed you, tell them what you saw."

Wentworth stooped and, on the forehead of the dead sergeant, ground in the seal of the Spider!

"The Spider!" the man gabbled. "The Spider! Oh, thank God. We have needed a leader—"

"Hurry!" Wentworth ordered.

When he turned back to the truck, Sailor Joe had already stripped off two of the uniforms and loaded them aboard. He stared at Wentworth with a half-frightened look in his usually cheerful eyes.

"The Spider?" he said slowly. "You... the Spider?"

"I know the Spider," Wentworth told him quietly. "He has given me the right to use his seal. It is something the Black Police can understand. Soon, you will be given the right to use that seal, too. Every man I can trust shall have that seal! We'll put the fear of God in these Black Police!"

Sailor Joe chuckled, though its note was a little uncertain. "Fear of God, huh? I'd call it the fear of sudden death and the Spider!"

Wentworth's lips felt as if they would never again relax in

a smile. He said curtly. "We have three minutes to make the rendezvous. And there is still the police payroll to be seized!"

CHAPTER 12
DISCIPLES OF HELL

OF THE eight men who had set out to acquire uniforms of the Black Police, six came to the rendezvous with their loot. The seventh reported to Wentworth, his face white and drawn.

"We got our men all right, sir," he said, "then an armored car came up. Martin was killed. I managed to escape—but without the uniform."

Wentworth's lips drew out thinly. "I'm sorry for that," he said quietly. "Martin will be avenged within the hour! You'll find an extra uniform in the back of the car. Hurry. Our time is drawing short!"

If the courage of any of the men was shaken by the casualty, they did not show it. Rather, they were more grimly determined than before. Wentworth hurried them all into the body of the armored truck and, Sailor Joe at the wheel, they sped toward the payoff headquarters of the Black Police. Wentworth entered the back with them.

"This should be simple," he said quietly, "but there is a fair chance that some of us will be shot, so play it cautiously. We will go into the headquarters in a body. As I understand the layout, there are two offices connected by a wicket through which the payrolls of the various stations are passed. The bulk of men will be in the outer room. Five of you, under Sailor Joe, will guard that room, from outside. Shoot anyone who tries to get out. I'll take the other three men and force the door on the payroll room. It will be better not to leave anyone in the truck, but, at the first shot, Sailor Joe will send a man to start the engine."

He looked slowly from face to face then but failed to detect any sign of weakness. A smile moved his stern lips. "You'll do," he said. "If anyone is hit, he is to be carried by the others to the truck. The chief risk will be for the three men who go with me. I'll ask for volunteers. Just raise your hands."

If there was any disparity in time among the unanimous lifting of hands, Wentworth failed to spot it. He nodded his approval and made his choice just as the truck slowed at the entrance of a barracks-like brick building. One of the Black Police was lolling in the door, smoking. No one else was in sight, but through a window, Wentworth saw a dozen uniformed men lolling about a large room. He frowned at that. Their getaway would be in plain sight through that window. It couldn't be helped now.

As he swung to the ground, he stopped to speak to Sailor Joe. "Take that man at the door," he said shortly. "Post one of your men in his place. He is to shoot anyone who shows at that window after we begin our attack."

Sailor Joe nodded calmly and the men climbed down leisurely from the truck. Wentworth moved ahead, stopping to light a cigarette before he went toward the entrance. He nodded to the guard at the door.

"Getting cold," he remarked and went on past.

The survivors of the gunfight would only know that men in

their own uniforms committed the robbery.

The guard grunted. "Damn cold, if you have to stand out here." He turned to glance at Wentworth and that was the moment Sailor Joe struck.

"Tuck this in the bushes," he said shortly to two of his men. "It won't be waking up any time soon." He singled out the man whose partner had been killed. "You stick right here and play guard. After the shooting starts, you nail anybody who tries to get through that window. Remember what they did to Martin!"

Wentworth was relieved to find the corridor empty and went straight toward the door which led into the paymaster's office. The three men he had chosen were at his heels and bunched behind him as he bent to the keyhole with his lock pick. It revolved silently and, hand on the knob, Wentworth lifted his head and looked about him. His three men were ready, guns in hand. Sailor Joe and the three men with him were alert by the entrance to the main room.

"All right," Wentworth said quietly. "Here we go. Don't shoot unless you have to. But don't hesitate if someone yells or goes for a gun. And shoot straight."

HE OPENED the door and stepped into the paymaster's office. Three men were busy counting out money at a long table while an armed guard leaned against the far wall. Wentworth reached him in a long stride and slammed his automatic against the man's head. He went down without a sound, and Wentworth wheeled toward the others. His men had followed suit and two of the pay-counters were down. The fourth man, the paymaster, shouted out a startled oath and snatched at an under-arm gun. Wentworth threw his automatic, accurately, and, as the paymaster slumped to the floor, Wentworth brushed some silver money to the floor.

"Damn you!" he shouted in a hoarse imitation of the paymaster's voice. "Look what you're doing. Now, pick up every cent of that money!"

Some one rapped imperatively at the wicket, and Wentworth caught up his automatic and reached the window in a bound, slammed it up. With his body, he blocked the view of the room beyond where his men were scooping the money into sacks.

"Don't be so damned impatient!" Wentworth snarled at the Black Policeman who had rapped at the window. "You'll get your money. It's a pity they wouldn't give me somebody who could do this kind of work, instead of punks who knock all the money on the floor!"

The Black officer backed up, lifting his hands. "All right, all right," he said. "I thought I heard somebody yell!"

"I yelled!" Wentworth snapped at him. "One of those damned fools dropped the money!" He slammed down the window, turned to his men. "Quickly!" he whispered. "This is going too smoothly. Something...."

Like an exclamation point to his words, a gun crashed out in the hallway. The last of the money was being thrust into the sacks. Wentworth reached the door in a bound. More guns were hammering out there now, the corridor full of their crashing thunder. In the front room, men were shouting and their feet stamped hard as they rushed for the door. Wentworth peered out. Sailor Joe and another man were standing back to each side of the door, guns ready, silent and waiting.

"Fire through the door," Wentworth called, "but don't empty your guns!"

Sailor Joe nodded, and began a deliberate fire.

A hand touched Wentworth on the shoulder, "All ready here, sir."

"Good!" Wentworth stepped out into the hall. "Each of you fire three shots through the door as you go past, but go past there fast!"

He raced along the hallway. "Outside, Joe, and cover that window. Man at the truck?"

Sailor Joe nodded and leaped for the door. Wentworth took up his post, and the money carriers leaped past, guns in hand.

Their bullets sieved the door. But the police inside were firing now. The last man, leaping past, stumbled and staggered against the wall. His gun dropped from his hand, but he reeled on, clutching the money bag. His right arm dangled. Wentworth caught up the weapon and kept his post, firing at deliberate intervals until his piercing glance showed that all save himself and Sailor Joe were on the truck. Then he sprang for the steps, slammed the main doors of the building behind him.

"Fast, Joe!" he snapped. "On the truck there! Fire at the window!"

A DISTANT siren was beginning to wail, but under the cover of the gunfire from the truck, Wentworth and Joe made good their escape. The moment they were aboard, the armored truck leaped forward. Once out of the immediate neighborhood, they would be safe. The survivors of that ripping gunfight would know only that men in their own uniform had committed the robbery. It would be hours before they learned that their own men were not responsible, and by that time this little band would be safe in the hills!

Sailor Joe squatted stolidly beside him. "Sorry about that shooting, Mr. Wentworth. Couldn't be helped, sir. Four of them got suspicious after that yell and were trying to sneak out the door. We blew them back."

The other man laughed and, even the youngster with the broken arm managed a smile. When they roared clear of the city limits and began the race for the hills, they began to sing softly. Wentworth gathered the money together.

"This will buy a lot of arms to fight the Black Police," he said gravely, "and help many a poor soul the Black Police have robbed. And about that next raid, Joe…."

The singing stopped and the men were instantly listening. Wentworth could feel their waiting. He smiled and there was pride in his eyes—pride in the loyalty of these men who were eager to risk their lives in his service.

"I don't exactly approve of these concentration camps," Wentworth said softly. "I was thinking we might smash one open and turn the people free."

For a moment after he finished speaking, there was absolute silence, then Sailor Joe threw back his head in a mighty laughter. The others joined heartily and raised a ragged cheer.

"We'll fight the Black Police off the map!" they cried.

IT WAS after midnight when, rolling up the mountain road toward the camp, they were challenged by the alert sentries. Wentworth's call lifted a cheer of welcome and, when they reached the camp, they found an elaborate table spread in the main drawing-room and the entire group assembled. And yet a tension held the room, waiting as the men filed in, one after another. Wentworth walked straight to the head of the table and poured a glass of wine which he lifted.

"To a hero who died in line of duty," he said quietly. "To Martin."

They drank that toast in silence, and Wentworth shattered the glass on the table's edge and set the broken stem upon the mantel above the great stone fireplace.

"Five thousand dollars will be given to Martin's heirs," he said then. "Dugan was wounded. A five-hundred-dollar bonus to him. Martin did not go unavenged. We will probably never know the casualty list of the Black Police for tonight. They won't be eager to publicize it, but at least a dozen of them died!"

Sailor Joe walked up to the table with his rolling stride, picked up a glass. "By your leave, sir," he said. "Here's another toast. I'm giving you, pals… the next man to die for the cause! And if it's me—hell, just split the five thousand among you and drink her up. Sailor Joe'll be drinking with you!"

They laughed then and thronged to the table, and not until then did Nita come to Wentworth's side. Her hand clung to his. Kirkpatrick crossed and laid a hand on his shoulder.

"Now what?" he asked quietly.

"Double the guards," Wentworth said grimly. "It's time to set up those lookouts on the surrounding hills with signal fires ready to light, in case of invasion. We must send a truck to Numbersville. I sent fourteen victims of the Black Police there.

And I think our best defense will be to press on with our attacks. A raid on the police armory in Burnton is in order. We must smash open a concentration camp, arm the prisoners and turn them loose to harass the Black Police. From now on, we must be doubly careful about admitting any new recruit to the camp. And a week from today… we'll take that ten million away from the Black Police in New York City. On the last day of their 'Save-a-Life' drive."

"It's an ambitious campaign," Kirkpatrick said slowly. "What about the Master?"

Wentworth shook his head. "When we have disrupted the Black Police, I hope he will be forced into the open. And when he is…" Wentworth's eyes met those of Kirkpatrick and the smiles that touched their faces were curiously alike, bitter with the promise of death.

KIRKPATRICK HANDLED the raid on the arsenal in Burnton, successfully. He returned with three trucks loaded with revolvers, rifles and sub-machine guns, together with ammunition. But three broken glasses were added to the one that stood on the stone mantel.

Wentworth conducted the raid on the concentration camp. He mounted himself, Sailor Joe and Jackson upon horses and they took with them a dozen men, all veterans of their previous battles. They walked ahead of the horses, shackled together like weary prisoners, but the locks of their chains were not fastened and, under his clothing, each man carried two revolvers and extra ammunition. A truck followed behind with a hundred guns and ammunition for those Wentworth expected to free.

Twice on the way to the camp they ran into roving patrols of Black Police but they escaped suspicion and marched up to the barbed-wire barriers of the slattern camp in late afternoon. Wentworth had spied out the territory with great care. He knew that there were twenty Black Police stationed here to watch over three hundred prisoners, but only a third of them would be on guard at a time. It was the mounted machine guns, lifted on wooden towers outside the fences, which gave them control.

There was a perilous moment at the gates when the two guards stationed there started forward to search the new prisoners. Wentworth and Sailor Joe drove their horses up so that they blocked out the view of the machine gunners and leveled their automatics at the guards.

"Keep your mouth shut," Wentworth ordered harshly, "or you die!"

Jackson swung down off his horse and disarmed them, thrust their guns out of sight under his coat. At his orders, the two guards marched inside the barrier with the twelve "prisoners"— and left the gate unlocked.

Wentworth dared not wait for the results there. Jackson had his orders. He was to take the two Black Police inside the nearest building and there they would be overpowered and bound. Wentworth wheeled his horse toward the headquarters building, outside the barrier, and Sailor Joe followed. They had timed their arrival carefully for a few minutes before the change of the guard. Already the armored truck, with the two extra men Wentworth needed for his plans, was trundling into sight from the woods road a few hundred yards away.

At the door, Wentworth and Sailor Joe swung from their horses and moved carelessly toward the entrance. There should be not more than eight men in the main wardroom; the others should be off-guard and asleep in the adjoining bunk-house. Wentworth stole a single glance toward the prisoners' barricade. Jackson and two other men in Black Police uniform were moving toward the gates. That would be two of Wentworth's men in the clothing of the overpowered guards. So far, everything was moving smoothly.

Wentworth pushed open the door and went in, with Sailor Joe close behind him. Instantly, he whipped out his automatic and covered the eight men. Three of them were just pulling on coats for the guard change. The others were ready, but lounging carelessly about, and they were taken completely by surprise.

"The first man who moves gets his head blown off," Wentworth said crisply. "Your entire camp is surrounded with my men. *The Spider speaking!*"

Sailor Joe was already in action. He reached the side of the officer-in-command, in two strides, and cracked his gun against the man's skull. "If you want the same medicine, punks," he said, "just wiggle a finger. That's all, just wiggle a finger!"

He snatched down shackles from pegs on the wall and rapidly linked the men together, gagged them. In the midst of the work, the truck snorted to a halt outside and Wentworth's two extra men came in with Jackson just behind them.

"Into the bunkhouse, fast!" Wentworth snapped. "No time to tie them up. We've got to change the guard on time. Slug them. Hurry!"

Jackson and the two men darted through the door into the next room. There was a slight scuffling noise, a single muted cry, and then they were hurrying back. Wentworth looked them over quickly, nodded.

"All right," he said. "There's no formality about guard change here. You four men just saunter out and go toward the four machine-gun towers. Usually, the men on watch start to climb down before you reach them. Keep an eye on each other. As soon as all four men have started down, shoot them! Jackson is in command. All of you wait for his shot as a signal. Make sure you don't need a second shot. If one of them manages to reach his machine gun, there'll be more broken glasses on the mantel. All right. *March!*"

WENTWORTH WATCHED them file carelessly out of the door, then drew his automatic and stood near a window where he could watch the four towers.

Two of the guards already had started down from their machine-gun towers, but the other two were slow. Wentworth saw Jackson and Sailor Joe quicken their stride toward those two. This was the dangerous moment. The guards would know their relief men and, once Wentworth's men approached closely enough to be recognized, the trick would be discovered. And still the two guards remained in their towers! Wentworth could see one of them dimly through the side window, and he slowly lifted his automatic. The first two men had reached the ground and were turning toward their relief. Jackson broke into a run, reached the foot of the tower for which he was heading. Without a moment's pause, he whipped out his automatic and fired straight up into the tower!

Wentworth nodded and, at the same instant, fired on the one guard that he could see—the one toward whom Sailor Joe was racing. There was a brief burst of shots, then silence. Wentworth threw a quick, comprehensive glance over the scene. The two guards who had descended their towers were prone on the ground. Jackson signaled with a wave of his hand that his man was taken care of. Sailor Joe was swarming up toward his objective and, a moment later, signaled also. Wentworth's shot had sped true.

On the instant, the men Wentworth had planted within the stockade, burst out of hiding and the work of freeing the prisoners began. It was furious, frantic labor. Wentworth and his men must be back in the hills before a report of this was made and the patrols took the roads. When the prisoners all had been assembled outside the gate, Wentworth mounted to the truck and addressed them.

"I have weapons here for a hundred of you," he said briskly. "You will know how to use them! Each of you will be given fifty dollars. Scatter as quickly as possible. I ask only one thing of you, in return for this. Fight the Black Police wherever you go. Some of you will fight your way across the borders of the state. Spread word as to what was done to you. And one other thing... Help each other. If you see someone oppressed by the Black Police, and can help him, do it. If a man comes to you from me, help him!"

Wentworth paused and a murmur ran over the prisoners, became a shout, a cheer.

"You will always know my men," Wentworth went on, more slowly, "for each one will carry with him a token—like this." He reached behind him into the truck and held up a scroll which he unfurled. On it was emblazoned the scarlet seal of the Spider!

The cheer that rose, then, echoed against the surrounding hills.

His men sprang swiftly to work. The crowd was shaped into two long files to which, as they passed the tailgate of the truck, money and guns and ammunition were handed out. Others of Wentworth's men were swiftly dismounting the machine guns, assembling ammunition and supplies. Two hours after the first shot had been fired, they were heading toward the hills and comparative safety. Behind them, the released fugitives were already scattering. Some would undoubtedly be recaptured, and Wentworth dreaded to think of their fate. But more would break free.

They were within a half hour of the camp when the radio brought them news that the delivery at the camp had been discovered.

"Governor Whiting has announced a new reward for the outlaw, Richard Wentworth, who calls himself the Spider," the announcer said. "To the ten thousand dollars already offered for his capture, dead or alive, the governor himself will add an additional fifty thousand dollars—dead or alive."

The announcer went on. "In the emergency, and because of numerous depredations by armed men, Governor Whiting has declared the state under martial law. Hereafter, any man carrying arms without proper permit, or found in possession of arms, shall be considered in armed rebellion against the state. The penalty for armed rebellion is death!"

A grim silence settled over the men in the truck, but Sailor Joe merely chuckled. "The way that guy says it," he said, "you'd think that was something new. Hell, the way I look at it, they can't do no more than kill us! And they've been trying that plenty already! My glass ain't broken yet!"

Laughter rippled over the men then and it was a singing, once more happy squad of men who tramped into the late dinner table in the camp that night. Only Nita's violet eyes were worried.

"Sixty thousand dollars on your head, Dick," she whispered. "Men have forgotten loyalty and gratitude before this for that amount" Her eyes searched and weighed the half hundred men gathered in the hall. "Oh, Dick, where will all this end?"

CHAPTER 13
MASTER OF MURDER!

THOUGH WENTWORTH smiled at Nita's fears of possible betrayal by his own men for the sake of the reward money, he knew the heavy temptation it represented. As long as they were winning, the danger was probably slight, but once let the Black Police gain ascendancy for a day or a week, and the situation would be reversed.

During the days that followed, when Wentworth was preparing for the attack upon New York City itself, he kept the men

153

busy improving their quarters and strengthening the fortifica-
tions he had thrown up about the camp. A half dozen times,
planes cruised low over the hills. At such times, all activity ceased
and men remained utterly motionless in the forests. Apparently,
they escaped observation.

The radio brought an increasing budget of disorders. The
men Wentworth had freed from the concentration camp were
striking on all sides. Black Police were waylaid in the course of
their duty; a chain gang of prisoners was freed; a sergeant was
hanged on the main street of Poughkeepsie. There were reprisals,
too. Some of the raiders were captured and hanged. A group of
ten was seized in a quarry hideout near Peekskill and taken to
New York City for execution in the public square. Their hanging was announced for the very day Wentworth had set for his
raid upon the extorted contributions in City Hall Square. He
was determined that they be rescued.

Early on the morning of that day, Wentworth assembled
his men in the great main chamber of the camp. His fighting
force numbered forty now and all of them had been tested in
at least one excursion against the enemy. They presented the
appearance of perfectly trained troops, their demeanor quiet
and determined. Wentworth felt pride swell within him, and the
confidence of his bearing increased. They were a pitiful handful
against the ranks of the Black Police, but their morale, the deadly
accuracy of their gunfire, made them picked soldiers.

"We will draw lots—" Wentworth began his talk—"for five
men to remain in the camp and supplement the Chinese defend-
ers. The rest will be divided in this way. I want five men to carry

THE CITY THAT PAID TO DIE

rifles. It will be their job to mount various roofs and prevent the execution of the ten men scheduled to be hanged. Five more, scattered through the crowd, will attempt to start a riot."

He explained. "The diversion they create will be the signal for our attack upon the guard placed around the money. Concerning the distribution of the remaining twenty-five men, I will give more detailed orders later. A rendezvous will be fixed on the northern boundaries of the city. If any man fails to make that rendezvous on time, there will be a secondary rendezvous and a car hidden for their escape. Any questions?"

None of the men stirred or spoke and Wentworth smiled grimly down upon them from his stand on the steps.

"If we succeed today," he went on quietly, "we will have struck a powerful blow against the Black Police—and won a thousand friends among the people. We will have laid the groundwork for overthrowing the entire crooked government. And you will have a chance soon to return to your homes. Remember that when we meet the enemy this afternoon!"

The cheer that went up was tense and subdued, not through fear, Wentworth knew, but because it was the restrained eagerness of men before battle. When they were loosed upon the enemy, they would strike terribly!

THE HANGING of the ten raiders was set for five o'clock in the afternoon and a new gallows had been built upon a platform at the south end of City Hall Square—a long gallows on which ten dying men could swing at one time! It was not accident that the gallows had been built near the collection booth into which the intimidated citizens filed to make their extorted donations to the "Save-A-Life Fund" and receive the telltale Purple Cross which had the amount of each man's "gift" stamped upon its back.

The campaign had all the outward trappings of a charity drive and, silhouetted against that grim gallows, was a representation of a thermometer, twenty feet high, whose high point registered ten million dollars! Every hour, a man in the uniform of the Black Police would mount a ladder beside that thermometer and paint the level of the "mercury" a little higher, creeping up now toward the ten million mark.

All day a long queue of men had shuffled slowly toward the collection booth. With the lateness of the afternoon, that line increased and there were hundreds, thousands of others crowded into the square, watching in sullen silence the slow rising of the thermometer that marked the enormity of the fund wrested from them by intimidation and coercion. It was a cold, blustery day, with thickening clouds overhead and, a little while after four o'clock, a thin scattering of snowflakes began to drift down. At that time, too, a hangman arrived and draped ten ropes over the gallows.

In that thickening crowd, no one would notice the arrival of twenty men in pairs, nor remark particularly that they all worked their way slowly toward the collection booth where the thousands of dollars, turned in that day, was kept—and the new-built concrete building behind it where the entire contribution, running now well over nine million dollars, was stored under guard. The men waiting sullenly in line to make their contributions did not resist when two men silently wedged

156

their way into the queue ahead of them. They were in no hurry to surrender their money in exchange for that hateful tin medal which alone could gain them temporary surcease from persecution. If these two fools were in a hurry, let them go first!

Wentworth had calculated his place in the queue to a nicety. He wanted to move into the booth at the same time his men opened fire on the gallows guards. It would not be long now. Already, the usual guard of mounted Black Police was assembling. At sight of them, an angry murmur ran through the crowd, but it was soon muted. Terror rode the people of the city too sternly. Wentworth had difficulty in maintaining the stooping, cringing posture he had assumed. Jackson, behind him, muttered an oath.

"Our time will come later," Wentworth reminded him softly. "Do you know if everyone is here?"

Jackson shook his head. "I've spotted a few people we know," he said, referring cryptically to their assembling force.

Wentworth let his eyes sweep the crowd. He heard a renewed murmur and saw the tumbrel of this new revolution trundling down Broadway toward the gallows. Time was drawing short. Within ten minutes at most, his men would open fire from the roofs of surrounding buildings—unless his plans had miscarried. It had been necessary to separate his force into units of two, send them to the city separately. But he could count on his men.

His mind returned fleetingly to Nita's warning of a few days before—the temptation of the sixty thousand dollars that had been placed on his head. He had given any of the men an ideal opportunity to betray him today. But he had no real fear. There was no reason for this nervous restlessness that goaded him, except the anxiety for battle. That was what Wentworth told himself, but there was a coldness that dragged intermittently up his spine.

He was glad that Jackson stood guard on his back.

The tumbrel had reached the gallows now and the ten captives were visible, their faces pale blurs against the gathering dusk. Abruptly, a brilliant light blazed over the gallows and Wentworth smiled grimly. The Black Police were determined that the crowd should miss no atom of this reprisal, but they would be sealing their own death warrant! From the loud-speaker attachment in the collection booth, from which exhortations to greater gifts had been voiced from time to time, a man began to tell of the crimes of the ten prisoners. He was driving home the penalty for armed resistance to the authorities.

WENTWORTH WATCHED the faces of the crowd. Anger there, but it was sullen. They were terrified. The hangings would have their effect… if they were carried out. Wentworth's eyes quested beyond the crowd toward the street and, abruptly, he stiffened. Wasn't that one of his men with the Black Police hurrying along beside the queue of waiting citizens? Jackson's hand closed on his arm from behind.

"The reward," he whispered. "That's Megley there with the Black Police!"

Wentworth swore under his breath. The speaker was talking on and on, and the queue was not moving at all. Over there by the gallows, everything was at a standstill until the speech was finished. He did not want to start the raid until the diversion at the gallows had been begun.

Jackson said, "I'll attend to this!"

Before Wentworth could protest, Jackson had slipped from his place in the line and was starting toward the tall thermometer. Within seconds, he was scaling the ladder beside it. Men's faces turned white and questioning up toward him, but Jackson's eyes were focused beyond them. He had a clear view now of the Black Police—and the traitor with them.

"*Megley!*" Jackson called sharply.

For a moment the man froze amid his guardian force of Black Police. That was what Jackson wanted. On the instant, his gun blasted in his hand—three swift shots. Megley's scream rose hoarsely into the dusk, and Jackson slid down the ladder, darted away into the crowd toward the gallows. The bullets of the Black Police sang toward the spot where he had been, but they were seconds late. A series of black smears that were bullet holes marked the bright new paint of the thermometer.

The speaker in the collection booth had stopped abruptly. Fear ran its trembling course through the crowd. Men began to shrink back. On the outskirts, a few began to run away. They had learned by experience what reprisals the Black Police could inflict. Wentworth held his place in the line... and then he heard the faint, whip-like crack of a distant rifle and over there on the gallows platform, the hangman collapsed with a bullet through his breast!

Black Police were violently pursuing Jackson. A squadron of the mounted officers urged their horses forward into the crowd in an attempt to locate him. But the distant rifles were making a steady crepitation now. Among the mounted gallows guard, men were dropping from their saddles. Part of the group guarding the collection booth, broke into a dogtrot for the gallows, striking callously through the waiting crowd, hurling men from their paths.

It was the moment for which Wentworth had waited. He left his place in line and walked quietly toward the collection booth. Attention was centered on the gallows and the confusion around it, and Wentworth reached the door of the booth without being noticed.

He peered inside, cautiously. Five men there, all of them crowded against the rear window to peer toward the gallows and the excitement. Wentworth sprang inside with two automatics in his fists and began to fire. Only one of the men managed to pull his gun, and his bullet went wide as Wentworth slammed lead into his chest. Outside the booth, other guns were blasting now. A glance showed Wentworth that ten of his men were closing in on the concrete storehouse which was a mere projection of the one in which he stood. Three of his men sprang in through the doors.

"Orders, sir?" snapped a cheerful voice, and Wentworth could have cheered at the matter-of-fact manner of Sailor Joe.

"Scoop up the money," he ordered swiftly. "Get other boys in here to go through into the storehouse. Grab all currency. Ignore anything else. The guard set outside?"

Sailor Joe nodded, winked. "Me and another lad had to crimp one of these nosey Black Police. It just happened he carried a sub-machine gun. If those Black Police rush us, a lot of them won't never rush again!"

Wentworth sprang to the loud-speaker and switched it on. "Your money is being taken away from the Black Police!" he said swiftly, and his voice went booming out over the crowd. "It will be returned to you, on the evidence of your medals within a week or two at most—and in a way that the Black Police cannot trace! Rise against your oppressors! Attack the Black Police on sight! They must be overthrown or our state will perish!"

He told them, "We must fly now! Your money is going to be given back to you instead of wasted upon the Black Police and their criminal masters. *The Spider swears it!*"

FOR A moment after he had finished, there was absolute silence outside where the crowd huddled fearfully in the smother of falling snow, then a cheer started. It was feeble at first, then it roared out irresistibly. It swelled until its volume shook the night and drowned out even the harsh hammer of blasting guns. More of Wentworth's men were darting inside the collection hut now, into the concrete chamber behind—and fleeing, moments later, with a heavy bag of money swung over their own shoulders.

"Cars on the east side of the park," Wentworth snapped, as they fled past him. "Shoot any man who tries to stop you! Quickly now!"

Wentworth crouched by the rear window. The shouting crowd was milling in the path of Black Police who were attempting to charge through the mob with their horses. One of them was pulled from his saddle, and his scream rose thin and piercing even above the mob roar. The rifles were still at their work, for

161

man after man pitched from his saddle. The gallows platform was empty now and, as Wentworth watched, he saw the tumbrel lurch into motion. Men swarmed swiftly into the rear of the truck with guns blasting in their hands—and they did not wear the uniforms of the Black Police!

A touch on Wentworth's arm wheeled him about. "The money's out, sir," Sailor Joe reported. "Better go now, sir."

Wentworth nodded. "Call off the guard outside. If necessary, they are to throw away their guns and mingle with the crowd. They know the rendezvous." He turned toward the door and a choked cry rose in his throat. A man in the uniform of a Black Policeman, his face smeared with blood, swayed on the sill. In his hands, he clenched a sub-machine gun.

"Freeze, damn you," he whispered. "Don't try to move. There's sixty thousand dollars on your head and, by God, I'm claiming it."

Wentworth had holstered his gun; his men were gone. And that gaping muzzle that could spit bloody death was centered squarely on his body. A single slight pressure on the trigger and he would be riddled with bullets.

Wentworth smiled slowly. "Go ahead and shoot," he said quietly. He was playing desperately for time, without hope, without any real plan. Sailor Joe, beside him, was tense. "Don't try it, Joe," Wentworth said. "We're licked. But remember this, copper. Killing me won't stop anything. The people have found out how to beat you now, by organization, and…."

His voice died in his throat. Over the policeman's shoulder, he glimpsed the face of Governor Whiting's cringing secretary, Glass. The man was smiling widely.

"Got you, Wentworth!" he said. "Now, we'll smash your band of criminals overnight. Go ahead, man, and shoot! This means sixty thousand dollars in your pockets!"

"Glass!" Wentworth whispered. "By God, I see it now. I should have seen it long ago—at the Capitol. You met me at the door and sent me away and, moments later, the Black Police came after me. Then, when the face spoke from the mirror—the face of the Master—he knew my identity! And yet you were the only one who had seen my face. Glass…you are the Master! You are the head of this entire government, this bunch of criminals. You're a great man, Glass!"

Wentworth could see the tautening of the man with the machine gun, confident now that the high command of the state was behind him. His eyes flickered a little, but Wentworth did not move.

"Shall I shoot now, sir?" the man asked hesitantly, and this time he half turned his head away.

It was the moment Wentworth had waited for. His draw was a blur of motion and the automatic blasted in the same instant it cleared the holster. The bullet drove the policeman backward, and Glass was carried with him. Wentworth lunged forward, firing as he went, and gun flame answered him from the darkness. It seemed to explode within his very skull, and then all consciousness blotted out.

WHEN WENTWORTH recovered consciousness, he realized that he was in an automobile speeding through a black night which was thick with falling snow. Sailor Joe was beside him, and at the wheel was Jackson. Wentworth pushed himself up, violently.

"Glass!" Wentworth whispered. "Glass, what happened to him? If he got away...."

"He got away all right, sir," Sailor Joe said cheerfully. "But we got you away safely, too, and that was a close thing. Also, we got away with the ten million!"

"Damn the money!" Wentworth snapped. "Don't you realize that man, Glass, is the head of the whole damned thing! If we killed him...."

Sailor Joe chuckled, "Well, sir, we did sort of kill him. We chased him to an automobile and then we wrecked the automobile. But when we got inside of it, there was nobody there. Only some clothes Glass had worn, and this note."

He handed the note over and Wentworth read it by the uncertain light of the dash.

My dear Wentworth:

If you survived my bullet, which I sincerely hope you did not, allow me to compliment you on your strategy. You will never see Glass again, my friend. It is a role which has outworn its usefulness, but the Master—the White Face in the Mirror—is still at hand. No later than tomorrow, we will locate and destroy your puny band. Adios.

The message was unsigned, but Wentworth needed no signature. His lips drew taut with anger. Obviously, the identity of Glass was a mere disguise for the Master. His real identity remained hidden. And tomorrow, the Black Police would attack....

Sailor Joe laughed again, "Plucky devil, ain't he?" he grunted. "But he don't know where our camp is, and he'll have his hands full in New York after the licking we handed them. Jackson, here, has recruited them gallows birds. They're driving their execution truck to Numbersville. We won all along the line, and we're going to keep on winning, you can bet!"

Wentworth smiled faintly, sinking back against the cushions. He lifted a tentative hand to his bandaged head. He had the Master to thank for that. What Sailor Joe said was, to a large extent, true. Rebellious mobs would keep the Black Police busy in New York, and if the Spider struck again, swiftly, they might drive the criminals out! With such loyalty as Sailor Joe and the rest gave, the Spider could not be defeated! They had won greatly. Even the Master had been forced into flight....

"I'll find the Master again," Wentworth said softly, "and when I do...."

"When we do," Sailor Joe growled, "there won't be a spot of skin left on him big enough to put a Spider seal on! You can bet your bottom dollar on that!"

POPULAR HERO PULPS AVAILABLE NOW:

ACE G-MAN
- ☐ #1: The Suicide Squad Reports for Death $14.95
- ☐ *NEW:* #2: Coffins for the Suicide Squad $14.95

CAPTAIN COMBAT
- ☐ #1: The Sky Beast of Berlin $13.95
- ☐ #2: Red Wings For the Blood Battalion $13.95
- ☐ #3: Low Ceiling For Nazi Hell Hawks $13.95

OPERATOR 5
- ☐ #1: The Masked Invasion $13.95
- ☐ #2: The Invisible Empire $13.95
- ☐ #3: The Yellow Scourge $13.95
- ☐ #4: The Melting Death $13.95
- ☐ #5: Cavern of the Damned $13.95
- ☐ #6: Master of Broken Men $13.95
- ☐ #7: Invasion of the Dark Legions $13.95
- ☐ #8: The Green Death Mists $13.95
- ☐ #9: Legions of Starvation $13.95
- ☐ #10: The Red Invader $13.95
- ☐ #11: The League of War-Monsters $13.95
- ☐ #12: The Army of the Dead $13.95
- ☐ #13: March of the Flame Marauders $13.95
- ☐ #14: Blood Reign of the Dictator $13.95
- ☐ #15: Invasion of the Yellow Warlords $13.95
- ☐ #16: Legions of the Death Master $13.95
- ☐ #17: Hosts of the Flaming Death $13.95
- ☐ #18: Invasion of the Crimson Death Cult $13.95
- ☐ #19: Attack of the Blizzard Men $13.95
- ☐ #20: Scourge of the Invisible Death $13.95
- ☐ #21: Raiders of the Red Death $13.95
- ☐ #22: War-Dogs of the Green Destroyer $13.95
- ☐ #23: Rockets From Hell $13.95
- ☐ #24: War-Masters from the Orient $13.95
- ☐ #25: Crime's Reign of Terror $13.95
- ☐ #26: Death's Ragged Army $13.95
- ☐ #27: Patriots' Death Battalion $13.95
- ☐ #28: The Bloody Forty-five Days $13.95
- ☐ #29: America's Plague Battalions $13.95
- ☐ #30: Liberty's Suicide Legions $13.95
- ☐ #31: Siege of the Thousand Patriots $13.95
- ☐ #32: Patriots' Death March $14.95
- ☐ #33: Revolt of the Lost Legions $14.95

DUSTY AYRES AND HIS BATTLE BIRDS
- ☐ #1: Black Lightning! $13.95
- ☐ #2: Crimson Doom $13.95
- ☐ #3: The Purple Tornado $13.95
- ☐ #4: The Screaming Eye $13.95
- ☐ #5: The Green Thunderbolt $13.95
- ☐ #6: The Red Destroyer $13.95
- ☐ #7: The White Death $13.95
- ☐ #8: The Black Avenger $13.95
- ☐ #9: The Silver Typhoon $13.95
- ☐ #10: The Troposphere F-S $13.95
- ☐ #11: The Blue Cyclone $13.95
- ☐ #12: The Tesla Raiders $13.95

MAVERICKS
- ☐ #1: Five Against the Law $12.95
- ☐ #2: Mesquite Manhunters $12.95
- ☐ #3: Bait for the Lobo Pack $12.95
- ☐ #4: Doc Grimson's Outlaw Posse $12.95
- ☐ #5: Charlie Parr's Gunsmoke Cure $12.95

THE MYSTERIOUS WU FANG
- ☐ #1: The Case of the Six Coffins $12.95
- ☐ #2: The Case of the Scarlet Feather $12.95
- ☐ #3: The Case of the Yellow Mask $12.95
- ☐ #4: The Case of the Suicide Tomb $12.95
- ☐ #5: The Case of the Green Death $12.95
- ☐ #6: The Case of the Black Lotus $12.95
- ☐ #7: The Case of the Hidden Scourge $12.95

THE SECRET 6
- ☐ #1: The Red Shadow $13.95
- ☐ #2: House of Walking Corpses $13.95
- ☐ #3: The Monster Murders $13.95
- ☐ #4: The Golden Alligator $13.95

CAPTAIN ZERO
- ☐ #1: City of Deadly Sleep $13.95
- ☐ #2: The Mark of Zero! $13.95
- ☐ #3: The Golden Murder Syndicate $13.95